A Beautiful REFLECTION

A Novella

by

Sarah O. Maddox

Published by

Olivia Kimbrell Press™

Olivia Kimbrell Press™

PUBLISHED BY: Olivia Kimbrell Press™*, P.O. Box 4393, Winchester, KY 40392-4393. The *Olivia Kimbrell Press*™ colophon and open book logo are trademarks of Olivia Kimbrell Press™.
*Olivia Kimbrell Press™ is a publisher offering true to life, meaningful fiction from a Christian worldview intended to uplift the heart and engage the mind.

Some scripture quotations courtesy of the King James Version of the Holy Bible. Scripture quotations marked HCSB are taken from the Holman Christian Standard Bible®, Copyright© 1999, 2000, 2002, 2003, 2009 by Holman Bible Publishers. Used by permission. All rights reserved. Some scripture quotations courtesy of the New King James Version of the Holy Bible, Copyright© 1979, 1980, 1982 by Thomas-Nelson, Inc. Used by permission. All rights reserved.

Original Cover Art and Graphics by Debi Warford (www.debiwarford.com)

Library Cataloging Data
Maddox, Sarah O. (Sarah O. Maddox) 1938-
A Beautiful Reflection/ Sarah O. Maddox
    200 p. 20cm x 12.5cm (8in x 5in.)
Summary: A very beautiful and conservative Christian girl from North Carolina and a handsome, sophisticated bachelor from Atlanta, fall for each other at a company convention, but soon discover they have different values and beliefs.
ISBN: 978-1-939603-29-6 (trade perfect) ISBN: 978-1-939603-28-9 (ebook)
1. Christian fiction 2. man-woman relationships 3. love stories 4. family relationships 6. Christian romance

    PS3568.M838 6620 4
    [Fic.] 813.6 (DDC 23)

A Beautiful Reflection

A Novella

by

Sarah O. Maddox

"As the water reflects the face, so the heart reflects the person."

Proverbs 27:19 (HCSB)

For Vicki,
My precious
East TN friend!

Love,
Sarah Maddox
II Cor. 3:18

August 2014

TABLE OF CONTENTS

DEDICATION
DEDICATION

I lovingly dedicate this book to my wonderful daughter, Melanie Maddox Redd, who is beautiful within and without.

During your growing up years, like the heroine in this story, you were a committed Christian, seeking to uphold Biblical standards in every area of your life. An outstanding basketball player, you were a Christian example both on and off the basketball court.

As an adult, you have maintained your Christian convictions as well as a standard of excellence in all you have done. The author of an outstanding non-fiction book, *Stepping Closer to the Savior*, you have a blog with the same name. You are a popular Christian speaker and leader in the Mid-South.

Nearly twenty-four years ago, you married Randy Redd. You have two precious adult children, Emily and Riley Redd.

We are so thankful to have a daughter like you! You are dearly loved!

PROLOGUE

PROLOGUE

SUSAN Strasbourg and Rob Stallings began dating their senior year at Morganton High School. They shared the same beliefs and values. Several years before she met Rob, during a True Love Waits ceremony at her church, Susan made a commitment to God to maintain sexual purity before marriage. She wore a Purity Ring on her right hand. Amazingly, Rob agreed to abide by her commitment. All through their six-year relationship, they were faithful to each other and to God. It was truly "A God Thing."

Susan lived and worked in Morganton; Rob taught at the university in Chapel Hill. Susan knew Rob believed they would eventually marry, and she thought they might, too. But an unexpected proposal shed new light on their future.

It was a lovely spring day in Morganton. The rhododendrons and redbud trees were in full bloom. Rob was in town for an educators' meeting. Late that afternoon he called Susan at her office, inviting her to dinner at their favorite restaurant, *Thompson's on the Square*. Since she had no other commitments, Susan accepted his invitation. *Thompson's on the Square* was the only eating place in Morganton that continued to use white tablecloths and linen napkins. The tables were always decorated with fresh flowers. When diners were seated at a table, the waiter would light the charming old fashioned lamp gracing the center of the table. Either a pianist or violinist, or both, provided enjoyable background music from seven until nine o'clock each evening. It was an enchanting place to dine, serving excellent food.

They arrived at the restaurant about seven o'clock. The violinist was already playing. When Susan saw how excited Rob was to be at Thompson's Restaurant again, she was somewhat surprised. It had been several years since they had eaten there. *Rob must really be looking forward to having his favorite Shrimp Alfredo*, she thought to herself. When the waiter brought a special dessert they had frequently enjoyed, he told Susan: "I know you will like this, Miss. Rob tells me you two have enjoyed this dessert for years." Rob grinned from ear to ear.

Susan suddenly noticed that the violinist had positioned himself directly behind their table. As she turned around to compliment his music, Rob reached into his pocket and got down on his knees. When Susan looked back, Rob was kneeling beside her. The waiters had formed a semicircle around their table. Shocked at these developments, Susan gasped. Her face turned "white as a sheet," as she stared at Rob in disbelief.

Holding a small velvet box with a lovely diamond ring inside, Rob said, "My dearest Susan, I love you with all my heart. I want to spend the rest of my life with you. Will you do me the honor of marrying me?"

Susan was speechless — unable to utter a word of response. She couldn't believe this was really happening.

When she didn't speak, Rob looked mystified! With a sense of urgency in his voice, he asked her: "Susan, did you hear me? Will you marry me?"

She honestly did not know how to answer him, but she didn't want to embarrass him further. Hoping her perplexing thoughts were not glaringly apparent, she told Rob, "Oh, Rob, you know I care deeply for you; and I know you care deeply for me, too; but this is a complete surprise. I think we need to talk about it, first. Let's go where we can talk privately. Okay?"

Rob's face had fallen. Susan knew he had to be embarrassed and dismayed. This was to be a night of celebration; instead it was a full-blown catastrophe. She felt terrible about the way things had turned out.

Rob slowly rose from his knees, closed the jewelry box and put it back into his coat pocket. Clearing his throat, he said to the waiters and violinist in a surprisingly calm voice, "Okay, folks, thank you for everything. Susan and I are leaving so we can talk privately. If one of you will bring us the check, I would appreciate it." He could not look at Susan; his somber gaze was focused on the waiters.

A waiter came immediately to tell Rob their meal was 'on the house.' Rob tried to protest, but the waiter was unbending. After assisting Susan in getting up from her chair, the two walked quickly out the door of the restaurant. By this time Susan was crying.

When they were settled in Rob's car, Susan told him, "Oh, Rob, I am truly, truly sorry! You know I would *never* want to hurt you like this! I really wanted to say 'yes,' but I couldn't. As implausible as it seems, I believe it would have hurt you more if I had said 'yes,' and we later determined it wasn't God's will. Wouldn't it, Rob?" She pleaded.

"I don't know, Susan. I don't think anything could ever hurt me more than your refusal tonight!" he answered emphatically. They rode in silence until they reached her driveway. Rob turned off the engine, unhooked his seatbelt and turned to look at her. "What happened, Susan? What on earth happened? Don't you love me? I've thought all these years we would get married. Didn't *you*? What's going on?" He questioned, sounding thoroughly bewildered.

Susan was still crying. She unhooked her seatbelt, and took his hands in hers. "Oh, Rob. I do love you. You know that. I have loved you all these years. But I have never known for sure if I would marry you. I think you would be the perfect husband for me. I would be so proud to be your wife. But we have not talked seriously about marriage. Yes, we've kidded about it for years; but never once have you *asked* me to marry you. I may be wrong, but I think you just assumed I would. Am I right?" Susan asked, feeling increasingly uncomfortable.

He was silent a moment as he looked away and sighed. Turning back to her he responded, "Yes, Susie, I guess you are right. From high school on I assumed we would marry. I believed you were God's gift to me for a lifetime! What *is* the big holdup, Susie? Please, please tell me," he begged, revealing his unmitigated consternation.

Susan took a deep breath before she answered him. "Oh, Rob, first of all, I don't know for certain if it is God's perfect will for us to marry. Do you?" She didn't give him a chance to answer, but went on to say, "Second, I know that I truly love you, but I don't know if it's the 'marrying kind' of love." Rob's countenance revealed his displeasure with her explanation. She continued. "I don't have all the answers for you tonight. Please let me pray about this. I really need to spend time with the Lord. Come over in the morning and we'll talk about it. Again, I am so sorry! I can't even express how sorry I am!" She leaned over and gently kissed him. Then she opened her door and ran up the driveway to her house.

The next morning Rob drove to Susan's house. He opened the car door, closed it, and walked slowly to her front door. He pushed the doorbell button and waited impatiently.   Susan quickly opened the door, smiled, and welcomed him in. He was not smiling. She knew the wounds of the night before were still festering. She asked him to come into the den for privacy. They sat on the red and blue plaid couch where they had spent many an hour. Most of those times had been enjoyable. This morning was not to be one of them.

Susan began giving Rob the news she knew he did not want to hear. She told him about praying all night, as she sought God's perfect will for her and Rob; then she began sharing her true feelings with him. She had realized she loved him as a dear and wonderful friend, but not as a lifelong mate. She went on to say, "Rob, my favorite Bible teacher once told us, 'If God wants you to marry someone, He will tell *both* of you.' I know you do not want to hear this, but God has *not* given me permission to marry you. I am so very sorry!" She covered her face with her hands as the tears poured from her eyes.

It hurt Susan deeply to tell Rob she could not marry him; but she knew it hurt Rob much, much more to *hear* her pronouncement. What a sad day for both of them!

In the years following their breakup, Susan often wondered: Will I ever find someone who loves me as much as Rob did? When the person God does want me to marry comes along, will I know he's 'the one'?

CHAPTER ONE
CHAPTER ONE

SUSAN Strasbourg stared at the Atlanta traffic through the windows of her shuttle. The last time she'd been here was on a middle school field trip to see the Cyclorama. That was fifteen years ago. She was overwhelmed by the sheer size of the huge metropolis. Surely it had doubled in size. *Where do all these people live and work*? She wondered to herself. *Big city life has to be very different from life in a small town like Morganton, North Carolina.*

For the first time since Susan had been employed by Hitchenson Enterprises, she was attending the company's national convention in Atlanta. *Am I really ready for this convention*? She asked herself. Whether she *felt* ready or not, she was there!

Hitchenson Enterprises was one of the largest, most respected corporations of its kind in the southeastern United States. The company specialized in financial counseling and insurance. Allway Insurance was their large regional insurance company. Founded by James M. Hitchenson, Sr., in the late 1970's, it had grown into a massive organization with sixty-two branch offices. Susan was the branch manager in Morganton.

She knew she worked for a great company; but she had heard rumors about the company's past conventions — about the drinking and partying and much more. Her friends had warned her about the guys who would be on the prowl. She was told to be especially wary of the married men, coming 'solo' to this event. Susan could not afford to let these negative thoughts cloud her thinking. This was one convention she needed to attend! She was to receive an award for the "Outstanding North Carolina Manager" of Hitchenson Enterprises. The past year had been the most productive year in the history of the Morganton office. Now Susan's diligence, faithfulness and outstanding management skills would be rewarded.

As she bowed her head in thanksgiving to the Lord for this honor, she finished her prayer by imploring: "Oh Lord, please help me at this convention. I feel so 'green' and unsure of myself. I don't want to goof up. More than that, O dear God, please help me not to do anything that will bring shame to you or to my family. In Jesus' Name, Amen." When she opened her eyes, peace flooded her soul. It seemed as if God were reminding her: "*I will never leave you or forsake you. Let all you do and say glorify Me.*"

IT took an hour for the airport shuttle to reach the downtown convention hotel. When the van pulled up to the front entrance of the Bellevue Plaza, a bellman came to assist Susan in retrieving her bags. He placed her luggage on the luggage cart, pledging to meet her at her hotel room. When Susan entered the hotel through the revolving glass doors, she was awestruck by the huge two-story lobby with its glittering chandeliers and massive mahogany columns. Beautiful floral arrangements seemed to grace every formerly empty space. She had to search for the Check-In Counter. Once she found it, the hostesses were very helpful in getting her registered.

She took her room key and headed for an elevator, soon discovering that the elevators went only to designated floors.

She entered the one going to the eighth floor. Once she found her room and opened the door, two handsome cherry, queen-sized beds greeted her. Each had a matching mirrored chest. The fabric of the bedspreads and drapes was a floral with predominantly coral and white flowers on a light coral background. There was a comfortable-looking coral upholstered chair in the corner of the room. Everything seemed to fit together perfectly. *They had a good decorator,* Susan thought. *This is terrific! I'm going to enjoy staying here this week! I feel so safe and snug!*

She was startled when she heard the bathroom door open and a girl appeared in a red housecoat with her head wrapped in a towel. The girl 'jumped' when she saw Susan sitting in the coral chair. Quickly she spoke, "You must be my roommate! My name is Sally Hendricks. I'm from Panama City, Florida. What's your name?"

Susan scooted forward in the chair and introduced herself: "I'm Susan Strasbourg from Morganton, North Carolina. So nice to meet you. Are you the Florida winner?"

"Yes, I am," replied Sally. "You must be the North Carolina winner! This is exciting!"

Just then there was a knock at the door. The bellman loudly announced his arrival to let Susan know it was he. Sally scooted back into the bathroom before Susan opened the door. When the bellman was gone, Susan kicked off her shoes and sat down once more in the comfortable chair. Draping her shoeless feet over the matching ottoman, she relaxed for the first time that day. Sally soon reappeared, and they chatted for almost an hour.

The Convention was to begin at seven o'clock with a seated dinner in the hotel's Main Ballroom. Susan chose a cobalt blue suit for this occasion, knowing that the color would complement her brunette tresses, her deep brown eyes, and her ivory skin. As she finished applying her makeup, she stood back to look in the mirror, still undecided about her hairdo for the evening. She finally pinned up her long curls into an intricate twist. Earrings with cobalt blue crystal insets completed her outfit. Sally had not finished dressing for the evening. She urged Susan to go on without her, giving her a 'thumbs up' as Susan opened the door to leave.

CHAPTER TWO

WHEN Susan arrived at the ballroom, other convention attendees were standing in the hallway, waiting for the ballroom doors to open. Not seeing anyone she knew, as soon as the doors opened, Susan headed into the grand meeting room. One of the many male greeters approached her, enthusiastically offering to assist her in finding her table. Learning that she was an award recipient, he led her to the reserved front tables. Together they looked for her place card. When it was located, she thanked him for his help, and set her black evening bag in the seat reserved for her.

She looked around in amazement at the voluminous hall in which they were to dine. The chandeliers were different from those in the lobby, but equally as elegant. The dark blue carpet was a perfect background for the beautiful arrangements of American roses and miniature calla lilies atop every table. Votive candles and round crystal beads were scattered around the centerpieces, creating a festive atmosphere throughout the banquet hall.

She wondered if she would know any of the other attendees. Sadly, she recognized no one. In the left front corner of the ballroom she saw a group which seemed to be growing in size. Curious as to what the attraction might be, she stood on her tiptoes a moment; she discovered it was a bar, obviously set up especially for this evening's event.

Soon she was surrounded by other future award recipients, none of whom were familiar to her. Each seemed eager, and yet somewhat unsure as to how to get acquainted with their tablemates. A mix of ages and sexes, there were several older men and ladies, while others of both sexes seemed closer to Susan's age. It was not long until all had located their place cards and were seated, busily sharing stories about the company. Susan felt at ease for the first time since leaving home.

During a lull in one of the conversations at her table, Susan glanced over at the next table. There were six men and two ladies seated there. One lady looked to be the age of her mother, and the other about Susan's age. Suddenly Susan realized that one of the men at the table was looking her way. He smiled, and she found herself returning his smile. He looked so familiar — she was certain she had seen him before. It suddenly occurred to her where she had seen him. He was Mr. Hitchenson, the President of the company! She could hardly believe he was the one who had been staring at her. She felt her checks getting warm.

Deliberately turning her face away from him, she asked the girl next to her, "Do you know any of the people at the front table? Isn't that Mr. Hitchenson, the President of our company?" Even though she now knew who he was, she needed an excuse to talk to her tablemate and take her focus from him.

"Oh, yes – don't you know? That is the Hitchenson family," she replied. "The old man is Mr. Hitchenson – he's the CEO of the company. That's his son, Jim, the good-looking blonde. He is the President. His mother is seated between him and Mr. Hitch. His sister is seated on the other side of young Mr. Hitchenson. I understand she owns a big share of the company, too."

"How do you know all that?" Susan asked, surprised at the extent of her tablemate's knowledge about the Hitchenson family. She had only seen photographs of them in brochures or in videos sent to the branch offices.

"I was here last year at the convention and sat at a table on the other side of the family. A longtime company employee filled me in. The young Mr. H. — Jim Hitchenson is, they say, the most eligible bachelor in Atlanta. But rumor has it that he is a Don Juan — a really wild one. He likes the women and they like him, too. They say he loves them and leaves them like crazy!"

"Well, you certainly learned a lot, last year, didn't you?!" Susan exclaimed with a surprised look on her face. Upon hearing her friend's detailed commentary, she determined not to look Jim's way again. He was definitely not her type! But when she took a sip of water and glanced over the top of her glass, those two blue eyes of Jim Hitchenson's were staring at her once more.

Feeling a little uncomfortable, she decided to go to the Ladies' Room. She asked the girl seated next to her to accompany her. As soon as Susan got up from her seat, Jim Hitchenson arose from his and headed her way. Susan was a few feet away from the table when he caught up with her. He said in a voice loud enough to attract her attention, "Excuse me, please. I am Jim Hitchenson. I don't believe we have met."

Susan stopped quickly and turned around to face him. He stuck out his hand to shake hers. Trying to muzzle her delight, she responded, "Oh yes, Mr. Hitchenson, I know who you are. You're the President of our wonderful company. I am Susan Strasbourg from Morganton, North Carolina."

"Then you're our North Carolina winner, aren't you?!" Jim declared. "Congratulations! I'll have the privilege of presenting an award to you later this week."

Susan was shaking inside, and the words tumbled out one after another: "Why, thank you. That will be exciting! I really do love working for your company. It is a wonderful place to work. I'm not trying to flatter you, I just like working there … "

He interrupted her kindly. "That is good news, Susan. I'm

happy to hear you feel that way."

She tried to calm herself as she replied, "Thank you, sir. And thank you for introducing yourself. I look forward to this, my first convention. So nice to meet you." With that, she turned to leave, knowing that she must not seem too gleeful or in any way flirty. That would never do.

As she started to walk away, Jim spoke again in a loud voice: "Oh, Miss Strasbourg, would you be kind enough to allow me the first dance tonight?"

Susan stopped at once and turned back to him, stunned at his request. She haltingly inquired, "Oh … are we going to be dancing here tonight?" It was hard to conceal her excitement.

"Yes, we are. And I'd like for you to be my first dance partner. Would that be possible?"

She knew she must answer him, but she wasn't sure how. She paused, and then replied, "Well, yes, of course it would be possible. Where should I meet you?"

"Just be near your table. When the music and dancing begin, I will come and get you. Does that sound workable?"

"Yes, of course. And thank you so much for asking," Susan quickly replied, hoping that he could not tell how ecstatic she was. She had just been asked to dance the first dance of the night not only with the President of the company she worked for, but also with the most handsome man she had ever met! This convention was turning out better than she ever dreamed, and it was just the beginning.

As she walked back to her seat, her knees were suddenly weak. She began to realize what had just happened. She silently asked herself: *If the week is going to be like this, can I really handle it?* She began to question her decision. After further contemplation, because she had already accepted his invitation, Susan decided to go forward with the plan. *After all, he is my boss. It will be just one dance, and that will be the end of it. I can always tell everyone in the office that I danced with the President of the company!*

CHAPTER THREE

CHAPTER THREE

SUSAN came back to her table and sat down. She forced herself to focus on something besides dancing with Jim Hitchenson. She noticed that the hotel china was bordered in blue. It perfectly matched the carpet. The silver, china, and crystal together provided an elegant setting for the meal. The first course was already on the table. A fresh fruit compote in a delicate crystal dish had been placed at the center of every place setting. The waiters soon brought the salads — wedges of iceberg lettuce covered with blue cheese dressing, containing crumbles of blue cheese. Susan thought hers was outstanding.

By the time the main course was served, Susan had lost her appetite. How could that be? Fillets were her absolute favorites! With the dance approaching, Susan was getting nervous. When she had eaten a few bites, she could eat no more. She picked at her food, pushing it to the rims of her plate. The cheesecake, topped with raspberries and dribbles of raspberry sauce, however, proved impossible to resist. It looked yummy. One bite enticed her to eat two more.

Why am I so nervous? She asked herself. What's wrong with me? I guess I'm excited about Jim's invitation. Who wouldn't be excited about the prospects of dancing with Jim Hitchenson! Once in a while, she glanced at Jim's table to see if he was still there. Interestingly enough, nearly every time she looked his way, he was looking at her. *What is it about him?*

Why has he captivated me so quickly? I must build up my defenses!

Susan convinced herself she must not give in to her emotions and fall for this handsome stranger. After all – wasn't he living up to his mode of operation — already asking her to dance with him? He knew how to 'break down her defenses,' and she must not let him. From that time forward, she focused on the men and women at her own table.

It wasn't long, however, before her table mate jabbed at Susan's side to point out that Jim Hitchenson was headed to the podium. When she looked up, he was standing behind the lectern, calling everyone to attention. It was obviously his job to welcome the audience to the convention.

His stage presence, his build, his mannerisms, his good looks — all worked their ways into Susan's heart. She seemed powerless to quell the thrill that was rising within her as she looked forward to dancing with this incredible man. Questions ran rampant through her mind: *What is wrong with me? Why can't I control my emotions? Haven't I always been able to in the past? What is so different about Jim Hitchenson?*

Gaining back some control of her emotions, she tried to concentrate on the evening's program. It included video presentations and an after-dinner speaker. Susan found it difficult to listen to the speaker. *Will he ever finish?* She thought. When he ended his speech, Jim came back to the podium to announce a short break. After the break, the dancing would begin.

Her heart pounding, she dashed to the rest room, only to find a long line in front of her. *What if I'm not at my seat when Jim comes to get me? What if he doesn't wait?* She thought. Not wanting that to happen, Susan chose not to wait in line, but stepped aside to check her makeup.

She need not have hurried. Jim didn't make it for the first number. In fact, Susan was beginning to think Jim wasn't coming, when she heard his voice behind her. "I am so sorry, Susan. I had to take care of company business. Let's hit the dance floor!"

"Oh, Mr. Hitchenson, that is fine. You didn't have to come get me at all."

"Are you kidding me, Miss Strasbourg? I wouldn't have missed dancing with you for the world!"

He took her hand in one of his and put his other hand at her waist. She could not believe she was standing so close to him. For the first time, she could feel his warm breath on her face. Then he spoke softly, "You are so beautiful, Susan Strasbourg. Flawless, like the finest china. How did you get this way?"

Susan blushed, not knowing how to respond at first. Then she weakly replied, "I guess God just made me like He wanted me to be."

Jim stepped back a little, as if surprised by her answer. Then he recovered and declared, smiling broadly: "What a lucky break for the whole world that He did!" Susan just smiled.

They danced in silence for a few moments. Jim interrupted the silence by asking, "Tell me about Susan Strasbourg. How did you get to be a manager for Hitchenson Enterprises?

She smiled and began the story: "Well, Mr. Hitchenson, during my college years, I worked every summer as an intern at the Hitchenson office in Morganton. After college graduation, I began looking for a job in Charlotte. Meanwhile, a friend of our family in Morganton called to ask if I would allow my name to be considered for the Assistant Manager's job at the Hitchenson Office. I really did not want to stay in Morganton. My parents had just moved to Black Mountain. I thought it was time for me to see the world!"

Jim seemed to be listening intently, so Susan continued. "To make a long story short, after praying about my decision, I came to believe this was the right thing for me to do. I became

Assistant Manager of the Morganton office. Two years later, Mr. Fallen, the Manager, died. I was promoted to Manager. I have been there for five years, and the rest is history."

"Are you glad you made that decision?" Jim asked kindly.

"Yes, I am. It has been a great place to work, and I've thoroughly enjoyed it. I guess seeing the world will have to wait a little longer."

"Tell me what there is to do in Morganton, North Carolina?" was Jim's next question. Then he added as an aside before Susan had time to answer. "Somehow, I suspect Morganton and Atlanta are very different at night."

"You are right, Jim. In the daytime we have beautiful Lake James nearby. But we don't have much 'nightlife' in Morganton. That's okay with me. I'm not exactly the 'night life' type of girl. I don't drink, or go to wild parties; and I don't sleep around. So Morganton fits me pretty well. I'm very active in my church and community. The Mental Hospital and School for the Deaf offer lots of opportunities for volunteering. Those activities, added to the responsibilities of my job, leave me little extra time."

Jim wasn't saying anything. He was gazing into her dark brown eyes. She wondered what he was thinking, and how he would respond to what she had just said. She knew in her heart, she must let him know up front the kind of girl she was. Hopefully, this would put a brick in the wall she wanted to build between herself and any young man who might try to make a 'move.' The music stopped. Jim stood there holding her in the dance position and shook his head. "I can't believe what you just told me. I don't know what I was expecting, but not that."

Susan took her hand from his and took a step back, not knowing what to do or say next. She broke the silence as she told him, "Jim, I know what you are probably thinking. How did I end up dancing with *this* girl? This lady is a first-class *prude*. And you would be right. I'm sure to most people in today's world, I am a prude. But I'm not ashamed of it. I guess you could say I'm happy to be the way I am."

At first, Jim was silent a minute or two. Then a grin spread across his face as he stepped closer to Susan and loudly exclaimed: "Susan, if you are a prude, you are the most beautiful prude I have ever met! Welcome to my world, *Beautiful Prude!*" Then he took her hand once more. "You are something else! I have never met anyone like you in my whole life. Most of the prudes I've known have *not* been good-looking! You are surely in a category all by yourself!" They both laughed at his strong declaration.

Susan quickly thanked him for the dance, feeling certain he would have nothing else to do with her during the convention. She stepped back and with sincerity told him, "I enjoyed dancing with you. It was a privilege to dance with the President of our company. I am honored that you asked me." She smiled and turned to walk away from him.

Jim reached out and gently touched her arm. "It was my honor, Miss Beautiful Prude. Now, could you indulge me just once more?"

Shocked that he had not moved away, and not having a clue what else Jim could want from her, Susan responded, smiling, "And how could I do that?"

"Save the last dance for me." Jim replied. Susan was stunned. He actually wanted to spend more time with her? What an unexpected and unbelievable development! She seemed powerless to keep him from knowing how thrilled she was.

With a slight grin on her face she asked: "And how will I know when it's time for the last dance?"

He smiled and said, "I'll come and get you. Don't wander off too far. It should be in about thirty minutes."

"Yes, sir, Mr. Hitchenson, I'll be here … Unless, of course, I get tired and have to leave," Susan teased.

He leaned forward and grinned: "You wouldn't dare do that to me, would you, Miss Strasbourg? You didn't dislike me that much, did you?" he asked, teasing her back.

"I didn't dislike you at all." She paused. "In fact, I like you very much, Mr. Hitchenson." His expression told her that he liked her *reply* very much, too.

She couldn't believe her own ears. She had told him the truth about her lifestyle and convictions so that he would not think she was an 'easy catch.' Now, she was boldly declaring how she felt about him. Silently she asked herself, *What on earth, Susan? What are you doing?*

Susan hadn't noticed, but Jim had stopped. He backed up close to her and whispered in her ear, "I like you very much, too, Susan Strasbourg. I *will* be back soon." A whiff of his masculine cologne wafted through the air. He looked good and smelled good, too! Jim walked away quickly, grinning broadly and greeting everyone in sight with a high five, handshake, or pat on the shoulder.

CHAPTER FOUR
CHAPTER FOUR

ALL her resolve. All her determination. All her nerve. All had collapsed in a moment. The wall she had started building had crumbled. Her heart had won over her head, and her emotions were ruling her mouth. She thought of a Bible verse she had learned many years ago from the twelfth book of Matthew: "For out of the abundance of the heart the mouth speaks."† For goodness sake, why did her mouth speak those words to Jim? Not for anything did she want him to know her feelings. Actually, she didn't even know her true feelings until the words came out of her mouth — and her heart.

How could I be so careless? So foolish? "Lord, please forgive me, and help me," she silently prayed. "I have made a mess of things. I am crazy about this guy I have just met. And the worst part is that he now knows it. Please 'un-mess my mess,' dearest Lord. Show me how to act. Show me what to say and do. Please guard my heart — and my mouth. In Jesus' Name. Amen."

It seemed like ages before Jim returned. When he did, he had not lost that grin. He reached for her hand and declared, "Well, here's my Beautiful Prude! Are you ready to rumble?"

Susan gulped, smiled, and muttered almost under her breath, "I guess so."

He took her by the arm and guided her to the dance floor.

Then he suggested that she listen to what the orchestra was playing. "Do you know that song?" he asked eagerly.

"Oh, yes, that is currently one of my favorites. I really like the music."

Jim stopped and said, "You won't believe it, Susan, but that is *my* favorite, too. I asked them to play it for this last dance. I hoped you would like it." They both laughed and began small talk as he brought her close to dance once again.

Soon Susan cautiously inserted into the conversation her train of thought: "Jim, now that you know so much about me, why don't you tell me about *you*. I would really like to know about your journey to the top of the company."

Jim began to talk candidly about his upbringing. He told her he had been brought up in a wonderful family. He pointed to his sister who had been seated beside him, with his parents on the other side. He told Susan about graduating from the University of Georgia and going to Harvard Business School for his Master's Degree. He confessed that all he had ever wanted to do was to work for the company, marry, settle down, and have lots of kids. Somewhere along the way, he admitted, he had gotten sidetracked. He never found the girl he wanted to settle down with for the rest of his life. Instead he had become a 'rather well-known bachelor' in Atlanta.

What was he really saying? Susan wondered. *Why did he conclude with that admission? Was he opening his heart to me at this early stage of our relationship because I was so open with him?* Here was a successful and wealthy, ruggedly handsome, bachelor with a marvelous personality — the man who has everything by the world's standards; and yet, he seemed to be insinuating that he wasn't satisfied with all he had — his present lifestyle was not his first choice.

At that moment Susan was drawn to Jim Hitchenson in an unexplainable way. She was falling for him as hard as she was trying not to. The more she tried *not* to care about him, the more she cared for him. She knew she should have paid attention to that red flag waving in her face when Jim told her he was a well-known bachelor. Instead, as he looked at her with such intensity, something was happening inside that seemed uncontrollable. *Was she falling in love with Jim Hitchenson?*

I must get out of here. I cannot stay here with Jim, Susan thought. At first, her feet would not obey her. She seemed unable to move. All she could do was return his gaze. Finally, she took a step backward. The words began to tumble out: "Thank you again, Jim. It's been a wonderful evening. One I shall never forget. You have made the opening night of this convention a very special one for me. Thank you for making this little prude from North Carolina feel like Queen for a Night. Good night, Jim. I'll never forget this evening!"

With that farewell, she started to walk away from the man who had stolen her heart. Why set herself up for heartbreak in even dreaming he would feel the same way about her? *Why would a 'man of the world,' a famous bachelor, fall for a small town, devoutly Christian girl? My world is a million miles away from Jim's in scope and characteristics.* She told herself. *He would never fall for me!*

JIM Hitchenson *was* falling for Susan. Unfamiliar feelings were surfacing in his heart. He asked himself some questions: *Why am I so attracted to this girl? Is it because she is the kind of girl I've been looking for all my life? Is right here in front of me a woman I could picture spending the rest of my life with? Do I dare even think that at this point? Why would this pure, guiltless, naive girl even consider spending her life with me? What am I thinking? She wouldn't consider it if she knew about my past!*

Suddenly Jim realized the night was about to end, and he did not want it to. He began looking for Susan. He found her exiting the door of the ballroom. When he was a few steps behind her, he called to her: "Susan, let me take you around Atlanta and show you the town tonight."

Just outside the doors of the ball room, Susan stopped and turned around. Her face mirrored shock at his invitation. He could see the struggle on her face as she clearly sought to find a way to politely refuse. In the end she said, "Oh, thank you, but no, I don't need to do that. It's been a long day. Besides, Jim, I've already told you I'm not a 'night life' type of person. I would just spoil your fun. Thanks, anyway. I truly appreciate your asking me. I'll see you tomorrow." She smiled as she started once more to move away, nearly bumping into some other people leaving the ball room.

Jim reached out to her. He took her arm and spoke in a serious voice: "I don't think you understand, Susan. I want to spend more time with you." Then he added, "I know you aren't a bar hopper. I promise you if we stop by a bar, it will only be to introduce you to some of my friends. I really would like for you to meet them and for them to meet you. We won't stay long." With a twinkle in his eye he added, "Afterwards, I would like to take you to my favorite restaurant for some dessert. Would that be acceptable to you?" Leaning toward her, coming very close to her face, his countenance beckoned her to agree.

Susan smiled, hesitated and said, "Oh, Jim. That is so sweet of you. Of course, I'd love to go to your favorite restaurant. But I just don't think it would be best for me to go tonight. Okay?"

Jim looked surprised by her answer. He sighed, and with a sense of resignation said, "Okay, Miss Susan. I tell you what. I won't push you on this. I'll give you thirty minutes to decide. That will give you time to put on something casual and give me time to take care of some business matters. I'll call you at eleven o'clock."

He stopped to add something else. "I do understand what you are saying, Susan. If you decide not to go, your job won't be hurt in any way. This is not a boss — employee thing; this is a friend-friend thing … By the way, what is your room number?" He recorded it in his phone as he walked away, seeming confident of what Susan would do.

CHAPTER FIVE
CHAPTER FIVE

SUSAN wasn't confident! A war was raging inside of her. Her head told her *not* to go with him. Her heart longed to continue this 'journey with Jim' that had begun a few hours ago. What was she to do?

When she got to her hotel room, she talked to her roommate. Sally encouraged her to go. Susan said, "No, I don't think I should. I don't know him at all. Since he knows I like him, that makes the situation worse."

Susan was truly conflicted. She decided to change clothes anyway. There was only one casual outfit in her closet. Quickly removing it from the hanger, she changed into her new red capris and matching top. She brushed her teeth, and freshened her makeup. Taking out the pins that held up her hair, she allowed her brunette tresses to fall to her shoulders. After a thorough hair brushing, she sighed and sat down on the bed. It was time to talk with the Lord. She sought His wisdom as she whispered her prayer: "*What kind of mess have I gotten myself in this time, Lord? Should I go or should I not?*"

Her prayer was interrupted by a knock at the door. At the sound, Susan's heart leaped. Was it him? What should she do?

She called out, "Yes, who is it?"

"It's your pesky friend, Miss Strasbourg," Jim replied.

When she opened the door, he was leaning against the doorjamb, tie off, shirt untucked, cell phone in his hand, grinning from ear to ear. "You look wonderful, Miss Strasbourg. You look like you are going on a tour of the town. Am I right? Or am I mistaking your casual attire?"

She grinned back, waving her hand at him. "Oh, Jim, I just don't think I should go." Jim Hitchenson looked more irresistible than she could have imagined. Her heart was pounding wildly.

"Now, Miss Strasbourg, wouldn't you like to have an escorted personal tour of our fair city? Where could you get a better one?" Laughing, he continued: "Before you answer those questions, let me tell you that it's a good thing you said 'yes.' I was going to stand here until you did."

"I don't believe I ever said 'yes,' did I?" Susan inquired, smiling.

"Oh, don't you remember. When I knocked, you said 'yes, who is it?'"

He laughed and reached for her hand. She offered little resistance. She seemed unable to refuse Jim Hitchenson's offer!

"Do you need a purse?" he quickly inquired. Nodding in the affirmative, she ran back to her room to get her purse. She checked inside the purse to make sure she had her wallet and room key. When she got to the doorway, Jim happily declared, "I believe all systems are 'go.' The car awaits us at the front door." Susan told her roommate 'goodbye' as she closed the door and joined Jim in the hall. They chatted as they walked to the elevator. Susan could not have dreamed what the next few days would be like.

JIM was such a confident guy. He didn't even walk like the other guys she knew. He just strode along. His way of walking fit his personality perfectly. He was a go-getter. There didn't seem to be a passive bone in his body. He was also very persuasive — something Susan knew all too well. Wasn't she standing in the elevator with Jim Hitchenson, waiting to go and get in his car?

She grinned sheepishly in response to his look of conquest. The questions tumbled through her mind, one after another: *What must he be thinking? Should I have accepted his invitation?* She began to worry as she thought to herself, *Oh, my goodness! What have I done now?* An opportunity to trust God's enablement stood before her. If she asked, God would give her the strength to stand for her convictions!

She was brought back to reality by the ringing of the elevator bell as it stopped at the first floor. Jim took her arm and escorted her out the front door of the hotel. Then he began to talk once more: "Susan, my North Carolina belle, I think I'll drive you around downtown and point out some of the sights of the city. Then we'll go to Buckhead. That's where my parents live. There's a little place I'd like to take you where some friends of mine hang out. My friend Tom is there with his girlfriend Alicia. If that is not okay with you, we won't go there. All right?"

As he pulled out his key pad to unlock his doors, Susan gasped out loud, causing him to stop immediately to see what was happening. She declared, "Your car is awesome! I love it!" She could not believe Jim's sports car! It was a late model silver Porsche — exactly the kind of car she imagined Jim would drive! Sleek, stylish and fast moving! He smiled at her words and gallantly opened the door for her. She could tell by his expression he was thrilled she had been so impressed with his new sports car. She decided not to share the fact that she had never before seen one in person, much less ridden in one!

Once they were both inside Jim's car and buckled in, Susan

knew she had to answer Jim's question about going to the bar. Her head and heart were locked in a battle. Her head told her she should *not* go to a bar, even with Jim. Her heart told her it was okay because she *was* going with Jim.

Wasn't it only to meet his friends? The struggle continued. In the end, her heart won as she told him, "Jim, I think I will just trust you on this one. You know I don't drink and I wouldn't want to stay long, but if you want me to meet your friends, I'd love to." Susan couldn't believe she was agreeing to go. Somehow, it seemed okay for her to do tonight. If Jim stayed very long, she would ask to leave.

In response, Jim reached for her hand. She couldn't believe how good and right it felt to have her hand held by him, a man she didn't even know yesterday! As they rode along, he would lift her hand in his to point out places he wanted to show her. At a stop light, he turned on the music. 'Their song' was playing on a CD he owned. Susan smiled and leaned her head against the back of her seat.

"You look like you belong there, Susan. I like having you there in that seat. I can't believe I found you."

Susan wasn't sure what he meant. She didn't ask. She just smiled and enjoyed the moment — a wonderful moment — sitting in the front seat of Jim Hitchenson's silver Porsche, holding his hand, listening to a song that they discovered earlier, was a favorite of both.

CHAPTER SIX

CHAPTER SIX

SUSAN could not have imagined what Jim was thinking when he told her he was glad he found her. This lovely lady sitting beside him had stirred his emotions deeply — that longing deep within him to find someone with whom he wanted to spend the rest of his life, was more of a reality to him than ever before. He was feeling something he had never felt. He didn't really believe in 'love at first sight.' So why did these questions keep coming to his mind? *Could it be that Susan Strasbourg is the girl I have been looking for all my life? Is the reason I have never found a girl like her because I have been looking in all the wrong places?"*

Never would he have thought of going to a small town in North Carolina to find the love of his life. She would be in a large city like Atlanta or New York. Never would he have thought a religious girl would be *the one* for him. For goodness sake, Susan was a virgin, by all accounts. How in the world would she ever consider a guy like him, who had slept with more girls than he could remember? Why was she even here with him tonight? Well, for one thing, she had no idea of his reputation in Atlanta or his past lifestyle. The truth was — she didn't really know him at all!

The light changed and the music ended. Jim stopped his musings, too. "We're almost to the bar. You're sure it's okay to go in? I don't want you to, if it will bother you," he assured her.

"No, Jim. I trust the President of Hitchenson, Inc. I know you will take good care of me."

"Absolutely, Beautiful Prude. Does that bother you for me to call you that?"

"No, Jim. I think it's very sweet," Susan said softly.

Jim came around to her side of the car and opened the door. "I think you will like Tom and Alicia. I know they will like you."

Jim took Susan's hand and led her to the back of the bar where his friends were seated. He introduced them to Susan. Their reaction to her was very positive. Tom offered Susan a drink. Jim suggested lemonade for both. Tom's mouth fell open and he started to say something. Jim stopped him. He knew what Tom must be thinking. Jim had never ordered lemonade or ginger ale if liquor was available. "I am going to honor my friend tonight; I am having the same thing she does," Jim told them. Tom cleared his throat and changed the subject. Jim slipped his arm around Susan. She did not move away. Lively conversation filled the next few minutes.

When Susan and Jim got up to leave, Tom and Alicia expressed genuine disappointment to see them go. On the way out the door Susan said to Jim, "I really like Tom and Alicia. They were delightful. Are they seriously dating?"

As he helped her into the car, Jim replied, "They have been together for four years. I think they plan to get married soon." He shut her door and moved quickly to the driver's side.

Susan was glad Jim did not see her reaction. She still found it hard to accept living together before marriage. She knew this was true for more couples than she dared imagine — it just was *not* going to be true for her. She believed marriage came first; then you lived together. That was the way she had always believed; and that was the way she would live her life. Walking down the aisle in a flowing white wedding dress was her dream

— and being a virgin was her plan. When she walked down that church aisle to be married, the man who stood at the altar waiting for her would know she had saved herself for him and him alone! Oh, yes, that would certainly be rare these days — but it was exactly what she planned to do. She quickly prayed silently, "Oh, Lord. *Help me never to compromise my convictions. I want so much to do Your will and Yours alone.*"

JIM fastened his seat belt and turned on the engine. "Now, Susan, I have one more place I want us to go before we get dessert. I have more friends who want to meet you. We won't stay long. We don't even have to sit down if you don't want to. I just want all of you to meet."

"Jim," Susan asked after a few seconds, "How do all these friends *know* about me? You just met me tonight."

"I called them and told them we were coming. Let's see … how did I put it? I believe I said, 'You have got to meet Susan. She is unbelievable!'"

"You mean you didn't tell them I was a prude?" she teasingly inquired.

"No, ma'am. I did not. But I did tell them you were beautiful … because you are!" Jim declared.

Pleased with his words, Susan whispered, "That's very sweet."

"Actually, if I could have put it on Radio 750, I would have," Jim added eagerly. "I would be happy for the whole city of Atlanta to know that this fantastic North Carolina girl is my date tonight!" They had arrived at the next bar before she could respond. Jim pulled into a nearby parking place. In a split second he was opening the door for Susan. "This place will not be as noisy as the other … I hope," he told her as they walked through the parking lot hand in hand.

He opened the door to the bar. Unfortunately, he was wrong. This spot turned out to be even noisier; Jim ignored it all, carefully leading Susan past the busy tables to a booth in the back of the bar. There Susan saw five people seated — three guys and two girls. They were all smiling. The guys stood as Jim introduced them. Grins were on every face.

"Honey, you are a beauty! Jim does know how to pick them," one of the guys exclaimed. Seeing that Jim didn't want him to say too much, he said no more. By the time twenty minutes had passed, they all seemed captivated by Susan. As Jim and Susan got up to leave, Susan took the hand of each, called each friend by name and recalled something about him or her.

Jim was shocked and thrilled! He could not have scripted it better. She was an amazing person! No wonder she won not only Manager of the Year for North Carolina, but Manager of the Year for the entire company — which, at this point, only Jim and one other person knew.

When they walked out of the place, Jim burst out, "Oh, Susan, you were wonderful in there! Do you realize you remembered every name and something about each one! How do you do that? I bet you have never met a stranger!" He was ecstatic. Stopping for a breath, he took her arm and blurted out, "Susan Strasbourg, I don't just like you a little, I like you *a lot*! How could I be so lucky to have you here with me tonight?!"

Susan did not say anything in reply. Her smile told him all he needed to know. He helped her into the front seat of his car. He started to shut the door, but changed his mind. Instead, he stuck his head into the car, and grinning, he kissed Susan on the cheek. She blushed, but it was too dark to see her face.

CHAPTER SEVEN

WHEN Jim had gotten into the driver's seat, he announced: "Now, I'm taking you to my favorite restaurant. And because you have been such a 'trooper,' you can have anything you want!" He smiled and winked at her.

"Well, isn't that nice and thoughtful, kind sir," Susan responded with a twinkle in her eye. "I tried to be on my best behavior!"

After a momentary silence, Susan asked, "What are my dessert choices?"

"Chocolate, caramel, or crème Brule," Jim answered. "What is your favorite?"

"Oh, anything chocolate will be fine with me," Susan responded.

"Me, too, Beautiful Prude," Jim agreed.

Soon they were turning into the parking building of a skyscraper. Getting out of the car, she saw that the elevator was nearby. Jim inserted a card into a slot beside "City Club," and the elevator began its ascent. The restaurant was on the top floor. They stepped from the elevator into a beautifully appointed hallway. Rich oriental rugs were scattered on polished hardwood floors; beautiful lamps were attached to each wall. The entire length of the hall was filled with large portraits framed elegantly in gold leaf antique frames. Jim explained that the men pictured were the 'movers and shakers' of Atlanta. Hanging near a door was a bronze plaque engraved with the words, "Buckhead City Club."

The maître de was very friendly. Obviously, he knew Jim well. He greeted Susan warmly, remarking on the lovely woman Jim had by his side. They were directed to a table alongside windows overlooking downtown Atlanta. Jim suggested they sit on the same side. She thought he wanted a better view of the city, but he really wanted to sit as close to her as possible. Before the waiter came to their table, Jim took her hands in his, looked into her eyes and told her how wonderful and beautiful she was. "I know you think I'm flattering you; but I'm not, Susan. I can't keep my eyes off you. Is that okay with you?" He asked. She shook her head 'yes.'

After the waiter had taken their order, Jim lifted her hands to his lips and kissed them gently. "I would rather be here with you than any other place in the world! You don't have to believe that, Susan Strasbourg, but it's true."

"I do believe you, Jim. I love being here. It's lovely. Thank you for insisting that I come." She broke the ice and kidded him a little. "You know you had to twist my arm to get me to come!"

"I noticed that you were very hesitant," Jim responded, laughing.

"Well, it seemed like a shame to turn down an evening with the President. I would be giving up such bragging rights!" she grinned at him sheepishly.

After they had chatted for a few minutes, the waiter brought dessert — a chocolate brownie with hot fudge sauce and vanilla ice cream for two. They each had a spoon. They dug in and began to enjoy their shared dessert. With each spoonful, Jim felt the attachment between them increasing. Their eyes locked as they sat in a daze until the waiter cleared his throat, and the trance was brought to an abrupt halt.

Susan began to chat with the waiter, politely inquiring how long he had been with the restaurant. From there, she moved on to asking about his family. Jim noticed that Susan always seemed interested in a person's family. She loved people and made them feel her love and caring. It was not a facade. He was seeing it with every person she met.

He noticed also that for Susan, there was no pretense or concern about being 'politically correct' or socially acceptable. She was just 'being Susan!' He was beginning to love and admire these aspects of her personality more than he was willing to admit. She was gorgeous, intelligent, an excellent manager — but she was so much more. She was the most caring, loving girl he had ever met besides his sister!

That was when he realized how much Susan reminded him of Violet, his sister. *Won't they like each other! Tomorrow night they can sit by each other.* He was planning to escort Susan to the big Awards Banquet. She would meet his parents, too. He knew they would love her. His mother would say, "Susan is a doll!"

Before they started back to the hotel, Susan took a trip to the Ladies' Room. As she passed a desk in the hallway, colorful brochures captured her attention. Adorning the covers was a picture of the dining room where they had eaten. She picked up one and began reading it as she walked down the hall. The byline under the picture read: "The Buckhead City Club is a private dining club with first class service and gourmet food." *This must be quite a place!* She thought to herself.

When Susan exited the Ladies' Room, Jim was waiting for her nearby. He did not want the night to end, but it was late; they needed to get back to the hotel. Tomorrow was a busy day for him! They were at the Bellevue Plaza before Susan realized it.

As Jim stood at the door of her hotel room, his emotions were rampant. This girl was not your average woman; she was a twelve, on a scale of one to ten. What was tomorrow going to bring? He didn't know. He just knew that tonight was a dream date for him. He thanked Susan for a fantastic evening, inviting her to be his date for the Awards Banquet. He could see she was thrilled.

He surprised her by asking her to come meet him at noon the next day. He told her his reasoning: "I cannot go an entire day without seeing you!" Not believing what she had heard from his lips, she agreed to come. He placed his hands on her shoulders and kissed her on her forehead. He helped her open her door. Thanking him again for the wonderful evening, she reluctantly said good-bye and entered her room. Jim walked toward the elevator with his head in the clouds. Tomorrow would be an interesting day!

SUSAN was exhausted, but much too excited to sleep. Her roommate, Sally, was sound asleep. She took off her shoes, reached for her laptop and carried it to the desk. The instructions for connecting with the Wi-Fi were conspicuously placed under the desk lamp. Following the instructions, she made the connection and got online. She wanted to know more about Buckhead, the place Jim had grown up.

She first performed an internet search for Buckhead City Club because she wanted to know more about it. She had never been in such a prestigious place! Among the things she learned was its location — it was atop the Atlanta Financial Center. Then she clicked on a website that had served the Buckhead community for many years. Several newspaper clippings caught her attention immediately. One clipping described Buckhead as a "shopping mecca," with gracious mansions and "elegant hotels." She found another website for shoppers. She was fascinated with the wonderful shopping available in Buckhead.

Lenox Square Mall and Phipps Plaza were both located there.

As she sat back in her chair for a moment, she thought to herself: *I am astonished that Buckhead is the place where Jim grew up! His growing up years in Atlanta had to be so different from mine in Morganton!*

Jim had told her a few things. He had lived all his boyhood years in the same "charming Southern home." *It had to be a mansion!* She thought. He had attended a private school where he played football and baseball. His parents had a strong marriage and were well respected. His dad was a lay leader in the Episcopal Church. Jim's family rarely missed a Sunday morning service at their church. *Is that all I can remember? Goodness, I don't know much about him at all! I definitely need to learn more!*

This was truly a different world from anything Susan had experienced! Where did these people get their money? She asked reflectively. Let me turn off this computer and go to bed. This is too much for a small town girl like me to take in! She closed her laptop and quietly prepared for bed. Tomorrow would be here soon!

CHAPTER EIGHT

CHAPTER EIGHT

THE first thing on Susan's mind when she awoke the next morning was her evening with Jim the night before. Immediately, she was filled with guilt for going to the bars. She thought to herself: *I made a big mistake. I got caught up in the thrill of being with Jim and meeting his friends. I need to pray!*

She quickly got on her knees and prayed: "Oh, Lord, I compromised my convictions. I am so sorry. Please forgive me. I was wrong to go to those bars. A bar is no place for a Christian to be! Give me the strength to be what You want me to be. I agree with that translation of Romans 12: 2 which warns us not to 'let the world squeeze us into its own mold.' Oh, God, I don't want that to happen to me. Please help me. In Jesus' Name, Amen." When she arose from her knees, she reached for her devotional book. Sitting in the coral chair, she began to read the day's devotional. How appropriate it was for her situation. She praised God that "His mercies are new every morning."

In a few hours Susan was dressed and on her way to meet Jim in the main auditorium. She was wearing a coral pantsuit that was a favorite of hers. She hoped Jim would like it, too. Her long curls bounced around her shoulders as she strolled down the hall. Suddenly, she realized she was walking too fast. She must slow down. Her outward expressions must not reveal her excitement within. *After all,* she thought to herself, *what is going on between Jim and me is probably just 'a short foray at a company convention.' I will leave tomorrow, and Jim will be a beautiful memory in my Museum of Memories.*

She stopped abruptly when it dawned on her that she had passed the entrance. Quickly turning around, she found herself standing squarely in front of two somber-looking female guards attired in the dark blue uniforms of the Hotel.

"May I help you, ma'am?" one asked without a trace of a smile.

"No, thank you. I am going in this door to meet Mr. Hitchenson. I have an appointment with him at noon."

"What is your name, please?" the guard asked a little too sternly. Susan gave her name, and the guard looked at her flip chart. "I'm sorry, miss, but your name is not on the list for any noon meeting with Mr. Jim ... So far, we haven't seen him meeting with any women. He usually has two or three girls on his arm by this time. This year, I haven't seen that, have you, Sally?" she asked the other guard. The other guard just shook her head.

Susan's heart sank. *Am I being viewed as 'just another of Jim's girls?' Does he make it a habit of latching on to women at every convention?* With those troubling questions swirling around in her mind, added to them was the possibility that she might not be able to enter this door at all. As she started to protest and try to explain the situation, the door opened and a man gestured toward her.

"Are you Miss Strasbourg?" he asked Susan. She nodded in the affirmative. "I'm Bill Sullivan, Jim's friend. Please come with me," he added in a pleasant voice. "Jim is waiting for you."

With the guard left stunned, Susan thanked Bill and walked through the door of the auditorium. She was relieved, but still troubled as she reached the place where Jim was standing with his back to her. Bill called his name and he turned at once to greet Susan. He smiled as he reached for her hands and grasped them with both of his. His gaze was mesmerizing. He soon realized that her countenance was not the same as the night before. He asked, with a worried expression on his face, "What's wrong, Susan? You seem upset."

"Oh, it's not anything important, Jim. I just had a little trouble coming in. I think the guard thought I was someone else. Everything is fine now."

Jim's concerned look was replaced at once with a joyful look. He told Susan he sent Bill to look for her in case she wasn't sure where to enter. Then he asked if she had gotten any sleep. "A little," she replied. "But that doesn't matter." She almost whispered, "I had such a wonderful time last night, it was worth losing sleep for."

He squeezed her hands and said, "I hoped you would feel that way. I had a hard time going to sleep myself. There was this beautiful face that kept appearing in my mind — beautiful face, beautiful eyes, and beautiful heart." He stopped and stepped closer.

"I've had four texts this morning from the friends you met last night. Tom's not a man of many words, but he sent a long text telling me how much he and Alicia like you. You cannot believe what an impression you made on my friends. They think you are fantastic! And so do I!"

All Susan could do was whisper, "Thank you. I loved meeting them."

At that moment Jim's cell phone rang; he reached into his pocket to retrieve it. When he saw it was his dad, he told her regretfully that he had to go. "When dad calls, I know it is important!" He reached for her hands again and kissed them. He thanked her repeatedly for coming to meet him. Smiling broadly, he promised to pick her up at six o'clock.

"I'm really looking forward to it," she enthusiastically called to him as he left with the man who had come to her rescue.

As she walked out the same door she had entered, the guard who had confronted her touched Susan's arm. "I'm very sorry, Ma'am. I didn't know. I apologize."

Susan smiled and patted her on the arm. "Oh, that is fine; you were just doing your job. It really showed me what a competent guard you are. I need to tell Mr. Hitchenson how good you are at what you do. Thank you so much."

The guard looked surprised at Susan's words; she stood speechless for a moment. When she was able to gain her composure, she mumbled, "You're very welcome, Miss."

Susan smiled as she left. Her spirits lifted. She turned her attention to the evening before her. *It may appear that I'm just one of Jim's girls, but I'm not. He likes me — really likes me — I know he does because he said so. I believe tonight is going to be a continuation of my dream.* With a free afternoon before her, Susan stopped to purchase a sandwich and drink at the hotel deli. Then it was off to her room for a much-needed nap. *I must not have slept at all, last night,* she reasoned. *I am bushed.*

CHAPTER NINE
CHAPTER NINE

WHEN Susan entered the elevator, a man was already inside. She barely noticed him. When she got off at the eighth floor, he did, too. She was not suspicious of his actions until she was a few feet from her door. He had followed her every step of the way! Not knowing what to do, she stopped abruptly and turned to face him.

"Are you looking for someone?" she inquired, nervously.

"Only you, beautiful lady. I have been following you around all day. Haven't you noticed?"

Trying not to display her instantaneous terror, Susan answered that she had not. Mustering all her courage, she hastily reached into her purse for her key ring on which was a container of Mace. With a stern voice she told him: "You must go, now, and stop following me. I do not want to have to scream or use this Mace. I will inform Mr. Hitchenson at once that you are stalking me!"

Fortunately, the man backed away saying, "I'm sorry; I'm sorry!" as he ran toward the elevator. Susan's hands were shaking so badly it was difficult to get her door entrance card into the slot. With that accomplished, she pushed the door open and closed it as quickly as possible. Her roommate was in a seminar. She would have to face this awful experience alone … *No,* she thought. *I'm not alone. God is here with me!* "Oh, God, thank you for protecting me. But what am I going to do?" The idea immediately came that she should call Hotel Security.

She dialed Security. With a quivering voice she told the security guard what had happened. He asked to come up to her room; but she declined the offer for fear someone else might get there first. He asked her to describe the man who had followed her. All she could remember was that he was short, black-headed, and wore a brown coat. The guard believed he had just exited the hotel by their booth. He promised to look into it at once.

She was now shaking so badly she could hardly stand. She undressed quickly, grabbed a robe, and plowed under the bed covers. Thoughts raced through her mind: Who was this man? How long had he been following her? How would she ever feel free to leave this room? She could not keep the tears from coming. Soon she had cried herself to sleep. The last twenty-four hours had been too much for this young North Carolinian.

About four o'clock, she awoke to the ringing of the telephone. It was Jim. "Susan, it's Jim. Are you alright?" She answered in a sleepy voice that she was okay. His words tumbled out, "Security notified Bill that you were being stalked. Security immediately placed a guard outside your door. Bill decided not to interrupt my meeting, so I just now found out."

"Oh, Susan, I'm so sorry. Are you sure you're okay? I can't believe this happened to you, of all people!" Jim declared.

"Oh, Jim, thank you for calling me. It was very scary; but I was truly relieved that nothing else happened. Tell Bill thank you so much for taking such good care of me."

"I will," he replied, still sounding unnerved. He was silent a moment before he spoke again. This time he seemed calmer. "Susan, I really need you to do something for me — I would like for you to change rooms. Is that too much to ask?" Jim asked gently.

"No, it's not too much to ask at all. I want to do exactly what you think I should do," Susan responded.

"Oh, Susan, I don't want there to be any chance of something else happening to you! I know it's a lot of trouble, but I'll send the housekeepers to help you pack. When you have finished packing, they will call a bellman to move you to another floor. If you can't be ready at six, I will come get you just before seven. Oh, Susan, I want you safe!"

They talked for a few more minutes. Shortly after she hung up the phone, there was a knock at the door. The housekeepers had arrived. They helped Susan gather her belongings and repack them. In less than an hour the bellman, the housekeepers, and the guard outside her door were walking with Susan to the elevator, carrying her things for her. When they all entered the elevator, the bellman inserted a key into the slot beside 'Penthouse.' Susan hesitantly inquired, "Sir, are we going to the Penthouse?"

"Yes, ma'am. You are going to be on Mr. Hitch's floor," he replied with a slight grin. "I think he is really worried about you, ma'am. You must be very special to him." Susan smiled, but said nothing.

When the elevator doors opened, Susan was surprised to see Jim's sister Violet. "Susan, I'm Jim's sister, Vi. He asked me to show you to your new room. Oh, Susan, I am so sorry about this." She kept talking as she guided Susan in the right direction. "We've never had anything like this happen at one of our conventions. Are you alright?"

"Oh yes, Vi. Jim and Bill have seen to it that I am protected. I am not nearly as frightened as I was," Susan stated decisively. Then she changed the subject. "It's so wonderful to meet you, Vi. Jim has told me about you and how precious you are to him. He has also indicated that you and I may have a lot in common. Thank you so much for being here right now." Susan hugged Violet. She felt so close to her at that moment.

Violet stopped at a door halfway down the hall. "This is your room," she told Susan. She gave Susan the key card and watched her put it in the slot.

Susan noticed that the guard was standing by. "Are you going to be up here on this floor?" she asked him.

"Yes ma'am, I am. From now on, you will be guarded at every moment. The Hitchensons are very protective of their employees."

"Yes, they are," Susan responded. "And how thankful I am for that. Thank you so much for doing this for me." She smiled and he nodded. As she and Violet entered the room, he again took his post by her door. He later told Jim he had never guarded such a good-looking woman. He could understand why Mr. Jim would want to protect her from harm. She was a beauty, if he had ever seen one!

Violet stayed for a few more minutes and then began to excuse herself in order that both of them could get dressed for the evening ahead. "Are you sure you will be okay by yourself?" Violet inquired as she started toward the door.

"Oh, yes, I feel very safe up here with all of you and with my own guard. Goodness, I've never felt so much like a princess. You-all are wonderful folks. Thank you so much, Vi." Susan concluded.

"Here is my cell phone number if you need me for anything," Violet added as she walked back to give Susan a card. "I mean *anything*!" She turned once more to go. Then she stopped suddenly and blurted out: "Susan, Jim really *likes* you. I've never seen him like this. I don't know if I should tell you, but he woke me up when he got back to his room last night to tell me all about you. He has fallen for you, big time. You better watch him — he can be a fast mover." With that she grinned and went out the door, closing it behind her.

CHAPTER TEN
CHAPTER TEN

SUSAN grabbed a chair and fell into it. At first she was thrilled by Violet's words. Then she felt a wave of fear clutch at her heart. *What did Violet mean when she said Jim was a 'fast mover'? Was she trying to tell me something? Is Jim treating me the same way he always treats a new girl he likes? No ... didn't she say, 'I've never seen him like this'? That would mean he feels differently about me. Or does he?* She leaned back until her head touched the back of the chair, as she cried out to the Lord in desperation.

"Oh, God. Please help me. I've been on an emotional roller-coaster ever since I arrived. I am so upset inside about the stalker; and yet my heart is so full of love and caring for Jim. Only You can straighten out my thinking. It is completely muddled at this point. I really don't even know how to act or react.

I keep seeing Jim's face and feeling his breath like a soothing breeze on my face. The way he looks at me just takes my breath away. All I want to do is be with him. Then I see the face of the stalker and I freeze in terror.

Please, God, remove this insistent fear that seeks to engulf me. I want to be engulfed by Your love, not by fear. Hasn't the Bible told us in the first chapter of Second Timothy, that You have not given us the 'spirit of fear, but of power and of love and of a sound mind?' May what You have given me triumph over these fears. I claim Your promise that You will never leave me or forsake me. I offer the sacrifice of praise … Oh, thank you, Lord. Please help me at this moment. In Jesus' Name. Amen."

Six o'clock came quickly; unbelievably Susan was ready. The knock at her door startled her momentarily; then she heard that familiar voice. Jim was here at last. She looked through the tiny window in her door. What a relief to see his handsome face. As she opened the door, he grabbed her and hugged her so tightly, she could hardly breathe. "I have been so worried about you. Oh, Susan, I am so happy to see you're okay. You look fantastic!" He grabbed her arms and pulled her toward him, kissing her on the cheek. For a few moments he held her as one who cared more than he had dared to let her know.

When the embrace ended, Susan assured him, "Jim, I'm fine. Really. Now that you are here, I am *more* than fine." Jim took her hands and continued to gaze at her. He wanted so badly to kiss her; but he didn't want to spoil her makeup for the evening. She looked perfect! He stepped back, smiling broadly.

Susan broke the silence. "Jim, you look so handsome — so wonderful in that tux. Oh, you look so good!"

What she had said obviously pleased him greatly. He responded, "Well, Miss Strasbourg, I guess we make a handsome couple, don't you think? Let's be on our way to the big ball." With big grins on their faces, the happy couple fairly waltzed toward the elevator. For the moment all seemed right with the world! At least in their world.

Violet opened her door as they passed her room. Jim offered her his free arm, which she gladly took. She joined them in their waltz to the elevator. As they emerged from the elevator on the ballroom floor, heads turned to look their way. What a spectacular picture they made as they strode down the hallway. The guests instinctively made a pathway for them to enter the ballroom. When they got to their table, the three were laughing and teasing, almost forgetting the horror of the afternoon's events. Jim's mother turned to greet the trio. "My goodness, what do we have here? The three musketeers?" she asked as she smiled at the three of them.

"Yes, mom, we have arrived," Jim responded. "And this lovely lady you have not met. Let me introduce you to the most outstanding award winner the Hitchenson Company has ever had — Miss Susan Strasbourg. Mother, this is Susan. Susan, this is my mother, Mrs. James Hitchenson, Sr."

Susan placed both of her hands around the hand Jim's mother extended to her. Five minutes later, Jim was pleased to observe that his mother seemed totally enthralled with this lovely girl who had come into their lives. He could tell by her expressions that Susan liked his mother, too. When for the next few minutes they chatted like two long lost school girls, Jim was convinced they had really 'connected.'

It was Jim who finally interrupted their animated conversation. "Mom, I am glad you and Susan are getting along so well, but she is *my* date tonight, you know. You'll have to continue this dialogue another time. Okay?" he concluded gently with a twinkle in his eye.

Ruth reluctantly let her go. "Oh, my dear, you are wonderful. I am so happy you came into our lives. Jim, this girl is precious."

"And beautiful," Jim's dad chimed in. He had come to greet his children.

Jim introduced Susan to his dad. Then he said, "Yes, mom and dad, I agree with you both about Susan. She is one very special lady!" He smiled at her, as he took her hand and bade them good-bye for the moment.

"I want you to meet someone," Jim told her as he once more gave her the look only Jim could give her. He was greatly pleased that Susan and his parents had "hit it off" so well. He wasn't worried about their liking her; he just hoped Susan would like them.

Jim took her over to meet his Vice President, Tom McNeill. He and his wife, Lillian were standing in front of a nearby table. "This is Susan Strasbourg," Jim beamed as he introduced her. "She is my date for tonight. Susan, I want you to meet my dear friends, Lillian and Tom McNeill."

Tom smiled and reached out his hand. Lillian shook hands with Susan also. Tom spoke, "I would say you found a real looker for your date tonight." Then he turned to Susan and warned, "But you better watch this guy. He is some kind of ladies' man."

"Oh Tom, don't tease her like that. She is just meeting us for the first time. Don't give this pretty girl a hard time." Lillian chimed in.

"Oh, that's all right," Susan responded, as she changed the subject to ask about their family. When they left Lillian and Tom, Jim introduced her to several other people. He wanted all his friends and fellow executives to meet Susan Strasbourg!

SUSAN and Jim were back at their table. He seated her beside his mother who was, needless to say, delighted to see Susan again. Placing her hand on Susan's wrist, she began to chat once more with this newfound friend. It wasn't long until the banquet began. Jim's dad went to the podium and asked the Chaplain of the company to give the invocation. Then he encouraged everyone to eat. After the meal had been served, Jim went to the podium to conduct the evening's events. His friend Bill came and took Jim's place next to Susan. It was clear they were not going to leave her without a man beside her. After this afternoon's brush with terror, they were taking no chances.

It was time for the Awards Ceremony. Susan checked her lipstick and sat up straight in her chair. Jim was again at the podium. He shared with the attendees information about the ceremony. Each state winner was to come to the platform when his or her name was called. The winners would be called in alphabetical order according to their states.

When he began to call out the state winners, there was much excitement in the room. Unexpectedly, when he got to North Carolina, he skipped it. Susan looked shocked. *Why would he skip over me?* She thought as she tried not to get upset. Noticing her reaction, Bill leaned over and whispered, "Jim is coming back to you in a minute. There is a reason he skipped over you."

Susan was surprised, wondering what was going on; but she masked her perplexity with a smile. Before long she heard Jim say, "And now for the winner of the award for the Manager of the Year of Hitchenson Enterprises — Miss Susan Strasbourg from Morganton, North Carolina!" He grinned as he looked down at Susan. "Would you please join us on the platform, Miss Strasbourg?"

Susan's hands went to her face. She was stunned! Bill helped Susan up from her chair and escorted her to the platform. As she mounted the steps, a thrilled young man, the younger Mr. Hitchenson, eagerly awaited her. "Congratulations! Miss Strasbourg! From what I hear, you truly deserve this award. Folks, she is a super duper manager. We at Hitchenson's are very proud of her."

The audience applauded loudly. Then Jim asked her if she would like to say a few words. Susan stepped to the podium and mouthed, "You didn't tell me." Jim grinned at her and whispered, "I couldn't."

Susan's acceptance speech included words of gratitude for a company whose byword was integrity. She also shared how much she liked being the manager in Morganton. The audience clapped heartily, seeming pleased with her short speech. As she started to walk off the platform, Jim stopped her to have a photograph taken. It would appear in the next company newsletter. Jim put his arm around her. She didn't move. To him, it was as if no one else was in the room but them.

No one else in that ballroom could have known what was in his heart; he truly hoped Susan felt the same way he did. Something special had happened this week — something much deeper and more wonderful than a national award for Manager of the Year. Jim believed their hearts had been knit together — whether for the short term or forever. Tonight, they were indeed a couple; and nothing could take away from the splendor of this moment ... Could it?

After the photograph was taken, Jim walked Susan down the steps where Bill was waiting. Bill was to be her temporary escort. He walked closely beside her. She responded to people's happy greetings along the way. When she and Bill arrived at their table, everyone reached out to touch her or hug her and tell her how excited they were. Jim had sent a note around the table, telling them ahead of time what Susan didn't know — that she was the big winner of the year. It seemed as if all were very pleased.

Susan sat down and looked at her plaque. "Bill," she quietly told him. "I already felt like a winner before this award was ever given. Not a winner for my work, but for the reception I have been given. People have been so wonderful and welcoming to me. I feel like the luckiest girl in the world!"

"That's great!" Bill replied.

At that moment, Jim went up to the podium to deliver the keynote address. He looked her way and smiled. She smiled back. Later on he learned that she had prayed for him constantly during his speech.

Often he would look Susan's way. No one else would have noticed, but she was focused on him every time his eyes traveled her way. When the speech had ended, everyone stood to their feet clapping loudly. Jim had wowed the crowd just as he had wowed Susan. He was indeed a passionate leader, and he had an even more passionate following. It was no wonder he was the President of Hitchenson Enterprises!

CHAPTER ELEVEN

CHAPTER ELEVEN

JIM started toward her table, but was intercepted by one after another telling him what a fantastic job he had done. Susan was about to sit down to wait for him when she saw a familiar face across the room — the stalker was in that banquet hall! She froze in place for a moment, then reached out to the nearest person for help. It happened to be the elder Mr. Hitchenson. Not able to speak, Susan just pointed. Finally, the words burst forth: "He's here, Mr. Hitchenson. He's here!!" Not knowing whether she was afraid or just excited about seeing an old friend, he tried to enter into her thinking. Then she added, "Mr. Hitchenson, it's the stalker. He's here!"

Bill had heard the last words Susan said to Mr. Hitchenson. Instantly, he was at her side, guiding her to the nearest exit. At the same time he motioned to a security guard who was standing a few feet away. He immediately joined them, guarding Susan on the other side. Bill told someone to get Jim; Bill used his cell phone to call Hotel Security. The ballroom was immediately secured. The entire hotel was in lockdown within a very short period of time.

Bill took Susan to the Green Room, and Jim soon followed. By this time Susan was almost hysterical. Jim entered the room and ran straight to her, taking her in his arms. She was shaking so much he could hardly hold her tightly enough to calm her. She began to cry while Jim talked softly to her. "We are going to protect you, Susan. I'm here. Nothing is going to happen to you.

Nothing, Beautiful Prude, nothing!"

The police arrived at the hotel quickly and the search began. They needed Susan to identify the stalker, but at the moment it was too risky. She told the Hotel manager he was short, black-headed, and wore a brown coat. Every man in a brown coat was rounded up. It turned out there were ten of them. They were escorted to a conference room and the remainder of the distraught crowd was released.

Two men remained in police custody after an hour had passed. Now, there was only one thing to do. Susan had to walk out of that room where she was being guarded, and perform a function only she could perform. Susan had to identify her stalker. The two handcuffed men were taken by police guards to a room with a small window in the door. Two more guards stood outside the room on each side. Susan was to look through the window and identify the stalker.

Jim held tightly to Susan as they walked down the hall. He could not believe what was happening. When they arrived at the designated room, the two policemen did not move. They looked solemn and severe. Holding Jim's hand, Susan very slowly and cautiously walked up to the door and looked through the small window. The suspects were facing the other direction. Barely above a whisper she told them, "It's the guy closest to the wall." As she moved back from the window, the guy suddenly turned and looked toward the window; but Susan was gone. Jim and two policemen were escorting her to a private exit where a police car awaited to take them safely to Jim's car.

WHEN Susan and Jim embarked from the police car and were safely enclosed in Jim's locked Porsche, Jim started the car and moved it forward a few feet away from the door where no one could see them. He put the car into 'park.' With the engine idling, he turned toward Susan. Reaching for her arms, he gently pulled her toward him, declaring softly, "Oh, Susan, you cannot possibly know how sorry I am about all this! Never would I have wanted this to happen to you!"

He moved back a little to look into her eyes for a moment. Then he cupped her face with his hands, so that he could kiss her. When his lips touched hers, he could not keep from expressing his strong feelings for her. She responded in kind. When the kiss had ended, Jim brought her head to his shoulder and almost whispered as he spoke, "Oh, Susan, nothing else bad is going to happen this weekend. I'm going to see to it that it doesn't. I will not let anything bad happen to you!"

Slowly he moved away from her, belted his seatbelt, and turned to drive the car once again. Attempting to brighten the mood, he exclaimed in a cheerful sounding voice, "Right now I'm going to get you away from here and take you to my favorite spot!"

"Oh, thank you, Jim, I'm so ready to get away from here!" Susan responded with relief in her voice. She fastened her seat belt before asking, "Are you going to tell me where we're going, or is it a surprise?"

"It's a surprise," Jim replied. "There is something I want you to see. We are going to the marina at Lake Lanier."

"Oh, you know I'll love that, knowing how much I love boats and water," Susan replied excitedly.

The moon was full. The night was beautiful. Jim was thrilled, but he could not have imagined how excited Susan would be. She excitedly told him the moon reflected on the water was one of her favorite things!

After she revealed this to him, she shared some things from her past. "My daddy taught me to love the water. He had a little fishing boat in which he would take me fishing on Lake James. After a day of fishing, we would cook the fish beside the lake.

Several of those nights, we watched the moon as it came over the Blue Ridge Mountains. When the moon was directly over the water, it caused the lake to glisten and light up like sparklers on the fourth of July. It was always a wonderful father-daughter time. You see, I was eleven when my brother was born, so I was an 'only child' for many of my growing up years. That meant many special times for just daddy and me."

"You have some great memories, don't you, Susan?!" Jim responded.

"Yes, I do," she replied. "And seeing the moon on the water like this is fantastic!"

When they arrived at the marina and pulled into a parking place, Susan noticed that other cars were parking next to them. Jim told her, "I hope you don't mind having guards around all the time, Susan. I just feel it's so necessary right now."

"No," she replied. "I feel like we have our own Secret Service. It helps me feel more secure."

When Susan got out of the car, Jim hugged her tightly, letting her know of his happiness with her. They walked hand in hand down the hill to the marina. Dozens of expensive yachts were docked there, all under the cover of tin roofs.

"I am going to see if you can pick out my boat, Miss Susan. It's parked in one of these slips," Jim told her.

"Are you going to give me any hints as to what it looks like?" Susan inquired.

Jim grinned. "You're on your own. I want to see how good you are at picking out what I would choose."

"Oh, me, Jim, that's not fair. I hardly know you." She stopped herself and looked at him sheepishly. "That's partly true and partly not true."

"I agree," he responded, as he shifted his arm and looked down at her. "In a lot of ways I feel like I've known you for months. I wish I had known you long before now."

"Me, too," she replied as she looked at him and smiled.

When they reached the docks, Susan asked, "Okay, which way should I go?" He smiled as he shook his head. Seeing that he wasn't going to tell her, she chose the nearest walkway and headed toward it. After she had walked past several boats, she turned back to Jim and asked, "Am I getting close?"

Jim responded, laughing: "No, Susan, I'm afraid you aren't anywhere near my boat yet. Maybe I should help you a little. Why don't we go to the *next* walkway?" Susan laughed as they turned around to retrace their steps.

Jim let Susan wander down that row without saying anything to her. At intervals she remarked about a boat she especially liked. All at once across the marina a huge yacht caught her attention. She stopped and exclaimed as she pointed in its direction, "Now, that's some boat over there! That's not a yacht, that's a 'yacht-she!' Who owns that beautiful boat?"

"Oh, someone from Atlanta," Jim replied, not giving her more information.

"Well, it's someone with a lot of money. That is the most fantastic boat I have ever seen! Daddy would not believe that one!"

By this time Jim was intrigued with her statements. "Somebody at your house besides you likes boats and water."

"Oh, yes, Jim," Susan exclaimed. "Our entire family loves the water. We are all boat people!"

She continued: "The city of Morganton is on the edge of Lake James, one of the most beautiful lakes in North Carolina. It is surrounded by the fabulous Blue Ridge Mountains. Water-skiing was a favorite pastime of teenagers in Morganton. Water-related activities were a way of life for my brother and me. Had Lake James not been nearby, Morganton could have been a boring little town tucked away in foothills of the mountains of Western North Carolina. Instead, it was a wonderful place to grow up!" Susan finished with obvious pride in her voice.

Not finding the boat on the second row, Susan skipped the third row and headed in the direction of the pier where the yacht was anchored. She stopped and took off her heels. She told Jim she couldn't continue to walk in her shoes — her feet were hurting too badly. With shoes in hand, Susan had started walking again when Jim suddenly stopped and said, "Wait, Susan, there is something I need to do."

She stepped back out of the way. What a surprise when Jim came over to her, pulling her close. He said in a whisper, "I need very much to kiss you right this minute;" and he did so gently and sweetly. She was flabbergasted but very pleased. Words came tumbling out of his mouth which she never expected to hear at that moment: "I love you, Susan Strasbourg! I love you and I love everything about you! Thank you for coming to Atlanta this week!"

Startled, she stepped back, looked into his eyes, and could only mutter, "Oh, Jim," as he pulled her into his arms and kissed her again. She could hardly breathe. She put her head on Jim's shoulder and reveled in what had happened.

It was at that moment Jim knew two things: Susan Strasbourg cared deeply for him, too; and he had found the *love of his life*! He held Susan tightly for a moment longer. Then knowing he would soon be past controlling his emotions, he pulled away and declared, "We need to go find that boat!"

"Yes, we do," Susan affirmed. Jim led her to the last row of boats.

CHAPTER TWELVE

CHAPTER TWELVE

"IT has to be on this row," Susan called out as she walked in front of him. "There aren't any more piers."

"Oh, I think we'll find it on this row," Jim said as he tried not to lag too far behind on the narrow corridor between the boats. When she came to the last boat on the left and Jim said it wasn't his, she looked flustered. Almost at the same time Jim said, "Look to your right," and he flashed the flashlight from his cell phone on the hull of the huge yacht.

Susan gasped as she saw in bold letters: "Hitchens II." "Oh, Jim, this is your yacht!" It's the most wonderful boat I've ever seen, and it belongs to you! How long have you had it?" She reached out and hugged him. He loved her spontaneous reaction.

"I've had it for five years, I think." Jim said. "I'm really glad you like it! I wanted so much for you to see it and love it like I do. It was something I always wanted; it was a happy day when I could actually afford to buy it. Let's go aboard."

Jim pushed a button on a gadget he held in his hand. A walkway rolled out from the boat and connected with the dock. Jim gently escorted her over the walkway and on to the boat. The lights came on when he pushed another button and soon they were at the side door. When they entered the great room, Susan was speechless. Then she declared, "I've never seen a boat like this. I cannot believe the beautiful decor, the awesome cherry cabinets, the massive stone fireplace, and the exquisite paintings. Oh, Jim, thank you for bringing me here. It is marvelous — just marvelous! I love seeing and enjoying what you enjoy."

Jim reached for her and brought her into his arms. "I am so glad you like it, Susan. I hoped you would feel this way!"

Thoughts began flashing through Jim's mind: *You will see it many more times, my dear, for I intend to marry you and this will become our Love Boat — our getaway — our place of precious memories — our children's favorite place.* He had to come back to reality or Susan would think he had 'lost it' mentally. Just standing there with that goofy look on his face was not the thing to do right now. He suggested they tour the rest of the boat.

Susan remarked favorably on every room. She told him, "Jim, it looks exactly like *your* yacht should look!"

When the downstairs tour was complete, Jim took Susan upstairs. As they stood on the top deck and looked down below, Susan commented, "Jim, my daddy would greatly love this boat. It was his dream to someday own a big yacht and take his family and friends sailing. He thought having a large boat was the ultimate. You have accomplished that dream and he would be so proud of you."

Jim was touched by what she told him. Slowly, carefully, as she turned her head to look around the marina, he came up behind her and put his hands on her shoulders and leaned his head against hers. "We will bring your daddy up here and let him stand right here. It would be my honor to do that for him." He kissed her ear and then her cheek. His arms moved around her waist and she covered his hands with hers.

"Oh, Jim, that is so kind of you to offer, even if it never takes place," Susan responded.

"It will take place, Susan, mark my word."

After a moment, Susan lifted her hands from his and started turning toward him. "Jim, we have talked several times about my dad. I would like for you to tell me more about yours!"

Jim moved back a step and responded, "Okay. I can do that. Let's sit on this bench a few minutes." As they sat on the bench, he took her left hand in his and began to share: "Toward the end of my senior year, some special counselors came to our school to give guidance on the transition from high school to college. On the spur of the moment, I decided to go and talk to one of them. I had never talked with a guidance counselor before; I thought it might prove interesting. I found a young man who wasn't counseling anyone. I asked if I could talk with him.

He introduced himself, and asked me to have a seat at a small desk. He sat on the other side. His name was Tom. For the next hour, I was confronted with the future ahead. Tom asked me some pertinent questions. Questions like: 'What do you want to do in the future? What do you want your life to be like?' He also asked about my specific goals and desires. For the first time in my life, Susan, I looked seriously at what lay ahead."

Jim shifted in his seat and continued. "This is the part of the story where my dad comes in. After Tom and I had conversed for almost an hour, I remember hitting my fist on the desk and saying something like this: 'You know, Tom, talking to you has made me realize what I really want my life to be like. I want to be like my dad! I want to find a girl I can't live without, get married, have kids, and be President of my dad's company! How does that sound?' I asked him,

He smiled at me and replied, 'That's good, Jim. I think you are headed in the right direction. Your dad sounds like a great role model!'

'He sure is,' I told him. "That's when I realized I hadn't taken time to let Dad know how much I appreciated him. When I got home, I went into his office and started sharing with him. Since that day, we have been very close. He is my best friend as well as the best dad anyone could want!"

Susan smiled and reached over to hug him. "Oh, Jim, what a wonderful story! Thank you for sharing that with me! I believe we both have awesome dads!"

"We do," Jim responded as he helped her get up from the bench. "I have something I want to show you. Give me your hand." He led her to the other end of the boat."

When they reached the opposite end of his yacht, Susan gasped in delight. The moon's glow seemed to engulf them. Everything was lighted up! The water was sparkling in the moonlight. Big tears welled up in Susan's eyes. "Oh, Jim, this just makes the bad things that have happened today fade away. It's like the light has displaced the darkness. *Thank you, Lord*," she finished barely above a whisper.

Jim thought he had heard what Susan said; but he had never heard anyone talk to God in that way. *How beautiful, he thought, to have that kind of relationship with God where you just talk to Him as naturally as you talk to a friend. I'll have to talk more to Susan about all this. My relationship with God is not like that. I wonder what she would say if she knew that about me. I'm a Christian. I go to church regularly. But, well, my lifestyle has not been exactly "Christian," I guess. But that is all in the past. I've turned over a new leaf. I've found the girl I'm going to marry and I'm a new man. We will get all that "religion" thing settled before she walks down the aisle. We have plenty of time for that kind of talk.*

They stayed on the top deck a few minutes longer trying to fully absorb the majestic scene before them. It was getting late, however, and Jim needed to take Susan back to the hotel. It was hard to leave this awesome setting; but they needed to go. They walked down the steps to the living room and prepared to depart. When they were ready to leave, Jim reached out to her, almost pleading, "You're sure, Susan, you won't spend the night here with me?"

"You know better than that," she said as he placed his hands on her shoulders and looked pleadingly into her eyes.

"May I ask you something, lady?" Jim spoke further. "If you did spend the night with guys, would I be the one you would choose?"

Susan laughed. "If I did — but I don't — if I would — but I won't — without a doubt it would absolutely be you, Jim." They laughed as they held each other for a long time.

Jim finally stepped back and with strong emphasis said, "Susan, you are the strongest, purest, cleanest girl I have ever known. I respect you more than any girl I've ever met; but I surely do wish you would change your mind on this matter!" He gave her a parting kiss.

CHAPTER THIRTEEN
CHAPTER THIRTEEN

TAKING her by the hand, Jim led Susan out the door of his yacht onto the pier. Neither said a word until they were back at Jim's car. He opened the car door for Susan and helped her get in. He was grinning as he opened his door and slipped into the driver's seat. Jim put the key in the ignition ready to start the engine. Then he took his hand off the key, shifted in his seat and turned to look at Susan. Taking her hands in his, he declared with great fervor, "You are not going home, tomorrow, I guess you know!"

Startled, she responded: "Of course, I'm going home, Jim. You know my ticket's paid for. My plane leaves at six-thirty tomorrow night."

"And the reason you have to be home tomorrow night is what?" Jim asked, smiling. "To put out the garbage? To feed the goldfish? To pick up your dog at the kennel?"

Susan laughed and replied, "Well, the dog is in the kennel and could probably stay a day longer. But Jim, the convention is over tomorrow, and it's time for me to leave."

"In my book, it will never again be time for you to leave." He sighed as he took one of her hands and brought it to his lips. They gazed into each other's eyes, seemingly unable to move. After a time of silence, Jim spoke again. "Have I pushed you too hard, Susan. Is that how you feel? Are you anxious to leave?"

Jim asked, looking seriously into her eyes.

Susan responded immediately, "No, Jim, I have not felt *pushed* — you haven't been pushing me at all. I am certainly not anxious to leave. But I'm not sure we need to spend more time together right now. Maybe we need to separate, catch our breath, and think things through." She turned away for a moment to reflect further.

"I don't like that 'sep-a-rate' part at all," Jim countered. "Can you tell me what it is we need to think through?" Jim questioned as Susan turned her eyes back to his.

"I don't have an answer for that, Jim," Susan replied. "It just sounded rational. And I haven't been too rational for the last forty-eight hours!"

She settled back into her seat as she looked out the window. "Normally, I'm a rational, clear-thinking, mature adult who doesn't make a move without giving it time and thought. But this week I've been walking in a daze, happy as a lark without a care in the world. You see, I met this wonderful man who has taken care of my every need, wined and dined me and made me feel like a princess. Only the Lord knows what the next step should be!" She put her hand on Jim's arm as she turned to look at him once more.

Jim laughed. "That's one of the things I love about you. You talk to yourself out loud so I can hear it. You are just a little bit crazy, you know it? And so am I. Crazy about you!" They rode for a few minutes in silence. Each was lost in his/her own thoughts. Jim spoke first: "Would you like for me to be the one to do something rational?"

"Oh, yes. I'd love it," was Susan's eager reply.

"Okay, Miss Strasbourg. As your boss, I would like to tell you that you are needed here in Atlanta until Sunday evening, when I'm sure we can arrange another flight home. We will find you a place to stay and furnish all your meals. A boat trip or two will be included in the weekend's activities. But before we can seal the deal, I need your word that you will spend all of this weekend with me except the time you are sleeping."

"And that's your *rational* decision?" Susan asked, not able to keep from laughing.

"Yes!" Jim declared. "Aren't you proud of me?! I came up with a great solution, don't you agree?"

"Oh, me!" Susan gasped. "You are really tempting me, now. I guess I can't disagree," Susan affirmed. "It sounds pretty rational to me!"

"It's a deal, then, lady. We are off to the races!"

Soon they were back at the hotel. When they entered the elevator, Jim put his key card into the Penthouse slot. They literally zoomed to the top floor. Everything was quiet. They tiptoed to Susan's room. After Jim opened the door to her new room, he held it open with his hip and leg, and grabbed hold of Susan with both arms. "Thank you, Susan Strasbourg, for being so wonderful ... and agreeable. You have made the right decision! I love you and I'll see you tomorrow about noon." With that he gave her a tender, lingering kiss and bid her farewell.

SUSAN closed the door to her room and leaned against it in a daze. Could this really be happening to her? Had she just agreed to stay in Atlanta and spend the weekend with Jim? Did he really, truly love her? The questions were bombarding her, but she was so weary, she couldn't think straight. The best thing to do was to get ready for bed. Sleep was what she needed! Yes, she needed to sleep on this!

Soon she was climbing into bed. She thought she would fall asleep; but the moment her head hit the pillow, the stalker's face appeared in her mind. The chills once again ran through her body and she pulled up the cover tightly around her as if to protect her from harm. *Who was he? When did he first see me? How long had he been following me? Why didn't I notice him? Why didn't anyone else notice him? What's going to happen to him?*

Her first impulse was to call Jim and talk about it, but she didn't want to bother him tonight. They would talk about it tomorrow. Just then the phone rang and another chill ran down her spine. She picked up the phone and softly answered, "Hello?"

"Sus, it's Jim. You weren't asleep, were you?" he asked.

"No, I just got in bed."

"I didn't know if you wanted to know about the stalker tonight, but the police left me some information. Do you want me to tell you about it tonight or tomorrow?" Jim asked kindly.

"Oh, Jim, I was lying here wondering about him. I came up with all sorts of questions I wanted answered — his name, where he is from, where he first saw me, etc."

"Well, here s what we know. His name is Landrum Trimble. He is manager of an office in Indiana. He doesn't have a record. He is married and this was his first convention. He has been in our employ two years. I don't know when he first saw you. The police said he kept saying 'I didn't mean her any harm. I wasn't going to hurt her. I shouldn't have been following her — she just looked so much like my sister who died three years ago. My sister was the most beautiful girl in the world, and this girl reminded me so much of her. I guess I was drawn to her for that reason. Please tell her how sorry I am that I frightened her and caused trouble for her and everyone else.'"

Susan was silent. Tears fell like raindrops onto the blanket.

"Oh, Jim, what will they do to him? I hope they won't be too harsh. He is just a grief-stricken, hurting man."

"Oh, baby, I don't know what they will do. That is something you must not worry about. I wanted you to know that about him so you would know that he was not a classic stalker or someone with a police record."

"Thank you so much for calling, Jim. That really makes me feel better about everything. Now, we just need to pray for him. He is going to have to suffer the consequences and that won't be pleasant. I'll pray for his wife, too. Oh, how awful for her!...Enough of that, Jim. It's way past our bedtimes. See you in the morning."

"I love you, Susan. Good night." For Susan the nightmare had ended; for Lan, it had simply begun. What would happen to Landrum Trimble? What would happen to his wife? Without a doubt he would be fired from Hitchenson Enterprises. What a tragic story!

CHAPTER FOURTEEN
CHAPTER FOURTEEN

IT was nine-thirty A.M. Susan awoke with a start. She looked at the clock and flung the covers off, hunting her slip-on shoes with her feet. *Oh my goodness*, she thought to herself. *I am not going to be ready by noon if I don't get going.*

She put on her robe, picked up her Bible, and sat in the upholstered chair once more. *What should I read this morning?* She had misplaced her devotional book. When she was looking for a place to begin reading, her Bible fell open to Psalm 127. The first verse said: "Unless the Lord builds the house, they labor in vain who build it." † *"Oh, Lord — why did You point me to this passage? Am I about to 'build a house in vain'"?*

At that moment, for the first time, the truth dawned on Susan — she didn't know *anything* about Jim's relationship with the Lord! She began to feel sick inside. She could not control the thoughts flashing through her mind: *Of course, he is a Christian. Isn't he? But his lifestyle ... if all those things I have heard are even half-true, he has not lived the lifestyle of a Christ follower. Oh, Lord, what have I done? I've let myself fall in love with a man whom I really do not know at all! Oh, I do not need to be staying here. I need to get out of here!*

Susan reached for the phone on the desk beside her, held on to it a few seconds, and put it back on its base. *On second thought, maybe that's why I'm staying two more days — to really get to know Jim — to know where he stands on spiritual matters, on social issues, and his political affiliation.* As she continued to reflect, it occurred to her that she had gotten "the cart before the horse," as her daddy would say. She had fallen for Jim first; now she would find out who he really was and what made him tick. *What have I done? Only a foolish woman would do that.*

Instinctively she turned to Proverbs to see what God's Word had to say about a foolish woman or any fool. After scanning a few passages, Susan fell to her knees.

"Okay, Lord. I'm in this up to my eyeballs and I don't know what to do. Would You please have mercy on me and pour out Your grace on me. I promise, Lord, I will obey You in this. I will not marry Jim Hitchenson if You tell me not to. I do not want to be 'unequally yoked'† with an unbeliever. I want only Your will for my life. I surrender to Your will. Speak to my heart, Lord Jesus — let me hear You clearly every moment of this weekend. May I be a blessing to all I meet. May I not give in to my feelings or my fears. Thank You, Lord. In Jesus' Name, Amen."

The ringing of the phone made her jump. Quickly she rose from her knees to answer it. It was Jim. "I'll be at your door at five minutes after twelve, Miss Strasbourg. Does that time meet with your approval?"

"Yes, sir. Good Morning, Mr. President. Did you sleep well?"

"Good morning to you, Mrs. President. Yes, I did."

Susan chose to ignore his greeting and told him she would try to be ready. They exchanged pleasantries; Jim concluded the conversation by telling her how happy he was that she had made the *rational* decision to stay. "It was a wise decision, Mrs. President. It is one you will not regret."

"I'm sure I won't," Susan answered, only partially confident that would be true when the weekend was over. "It is going to be so much fun!" she added, trying not to reveal her apprehension.

"See you in a few. By the way, I want you to know that I still love you. Is that a rational thing to say?"

"It's the most rational thing I've heard all morning."

At exactly three minutes after twelve, there was a knock at the door. Susan went to the door and looked through the safety window. Before opening it and asking who was there, she chided him playfully, "You are two minutes early. Are you a little overanxious?" She waited to hear his voice.

"Absolutely. I am ready for this day to begin!" At that, she opened the door to find Jim standing by a luggage rack, ready to take her bags to his car. Earlier she had realized she had a rather big problem. Almost all the clothes she had brought were dressy — suitable for a convention, not a leisurely weekend. She had brought one casual outfit which she wore when Jim took her out on the town; but she had brought no shorts or swimsuits.

The luggage barely fit in Jim's classy silver sports car. He had to pile the back seat to the ceiling. When they had gone a short distance, Susan told him of her dilemma.

"Jim, I realized something when I was packing. I didn't bring but one casual outfit. Is there a store where I might find a bathing suit and some shorts?"

"Well, Susan, being the rational thinker that we know I am, I've already thought of the fact that you might need to go shopping. I called my sister Vi; she suggested a store and told me the clerk to ask for. By the way, she insisted that you stay with her tonight and tomorrow night. How does that suit you?"

"Oh, I'd love that. That is wonderful. I had wanted to get to know her better, but there wasn't time. This will be great; but are you sure I won't be a bother? Did she have to change her plans for me?"

"No, actually, she asked me if you could before I asked her

if she would! She really likes you and wants to get to know you better. You'll have a ball together — you are like two peas in a pod." As an afterthought, Jim said: "Maybe that's one reason I was so attracted to you. You reminded me of my sister whom I dearly love and admire ... Um-mm ... I hadn't thought of that before ... "

AS they rode along, they conversed about the scenery and talked about Jim's boat. The traffic in Atlanta was horrendous to Susan; she didn't want to distract Jim. Eight lanes of traffic going each way. My goodness! They were in a race! A race to survive without having a wreck! Jim was using his GPS to find the store's location. Surprisingly, he was a very careful driver.

They soon rounded a corner, and caught sight of the store. He pulled into the store's parking lot and found a parking space away from the other cars. Turning off the engine, he turned to Susan and said: "Now, Beautiful Prude — I haven't called you that in a while, have I? — I want you to buy as many bathing suits as you like, and all the shorts and shirts you need. The bill will be paid by me – don't even think about arguing about this. It's something I want very much to do. Okay?"

Before Susan could protest, Jim had gotten out of the car. When he opened her door, Susan blurted out: "I don't know if I can handle all this, Jim. I am so used to taking care of myself. I am a 'tight wad' at heart. It will be hard for me to pick out very much, knowing that someone else is paying for it."

"My Beautiful Prude, get used to it! I would rather buy something for you than anyone else in the world! You will just have to let me have my way in this ... please. And I want you to buy the suits you like best. Plus everything else you would like to have for the boat or sports, etc. Okay, lady?"

"Yes, sir. I hear you. I will try to do my best."

Jim found the clerk, turned Susan over to her, and sat in a chair near the window. When Susan began looking at the bathing suits, she wanted to run out of the store. Were bikini's all they had? When she did not seem interested in the bikinis, the clerk led Susan to the two-piece and few one-piece suits they had in their inventory. There were two one-piece suits that caught her attention — a blue one and a pink one. She quickly pulled those from the rack and gave them to the clerk. The clerk looked surprised at her choice of one-piece suits, but said nothing.

There were dozens of beautiful shorts and Capri sets. Susan had never seen so many in one place. She looked carefully at the selections in her size and chose two shorts sets and two Capri sets. Now it was time to try them on. When the clerk came back, she told her Jim would love for her to model the clothes for him, if she didn't mind. Susan wasn't sure about that at first; then she realized he was paying for them. It would be good if he liked what he paid for.

She put on the pink suit. It fit perfectly, but she wasn't sure about the color. She decided to try on the blue one and then decide which to model. There was no doubt about which was the one for her. The clerk let out a gasp when Susan started out the door and said, "Oh, honey that is perfect for you!"

When Jim saw her, he whistled! "Man, you are beautiful! That one, you must have!"

Susan told him that was her first choice, and yes, she would love to have it. She was glad Jim didn't comment on the fact it wasn't a bikini. Susan chose two shorts outfits and one Capri outfit. She modeled the latter and showed Jim the others. He gave her his wholehearted approval. The clerk suggested sandals to match the two outfits and jewelry for all. Susan declined some of the matching jewelry when she found pieces that would go with more than one outfit. It was so hard to let Jim pay for this;

but she knew she must. Hopefully he would be proud of her for not scrimping.

They headed for Violet's house after they left the store. Jim couldn't keep it in any longer: "Susan, I've got to tell you. I think I will have to get a body guard to keep away the guys. When they see you in that suit, oh, man. My friends are going to be green with envy!"

Susan leaned over, touched his arm and kissed him on the cheek. "Thank you, Jim. Thank you for all my lovely things. Thank you for everything. I must be the luckiest girl in the world! I just can't believe all this. You are one special guy!!" She leaned further and kissed him quickly on the edge of his lower lip. Jim just grinned and looked straight ahead at the heavy traffic.

Soon they were at Violet's. Jim walked her to the door and rang the bell. As they waited for Violet to come to the door, Jim told her, "I will be back in a few minutes. I need a new swimsuit, too. We are low on groceries for the boat, so I'll need to go by Publix. I should be back in a couple of hours."

Violet opened the door and welcomed them in. Jim didn't go in, but kissed Susan good-bye and made his exit. Susan and Violet had the house all to themselves.

CHAPTER FIFTEEN
CHAPTER FIFTEEN

AFTER showing Violet her purchases, Susan sat down on the bed beside her, and girl talk officially began. With a huge smile on her face Violet told her, "I am so excited about you and Jim that I can hardly contain my enthusiasm; I have never, ever seen him like this! Susan, he cares more for you than for anyone he has ever dated. I know him very well; I know his MO. This is so different. It just thrills me to death. There is no one he has ever dated that I would rather see him flipped over than you." She leaned over and hugged Susan. "You are exactly the kind of person I've always wanted Jim to marry. I never thought he would be able to find someone like you."

"Oh, Vi, that is so sweet and kind of you," Susan responded. "I think Jim is wonderful. He has treated me like a queen. He has respected my wishes and been so protective of me. I've never felt so cared for in my life. And I care more for Jim than anyone I've ever dated. I don't know how I could have fallen so hard so quickly. I really tried not to.

Before I ever came to Atlanta, I gave myself several 'talks' on what not to do at a convention. The number one thing on my list was: 'Do not let yourself fall for anyone. Keep your guard up. There will be men *on the prowl*. Do not be taken in by their attention and niceness.' I don't think I was 'taken in' by Jim at all. Nor do I think he was 'on the prowl.' He gave me extraordinary attention, and I responded in kind. We just seemed to be drawn to each other. I kept trying not to fall for him. The harder I tried, the more I fell for him. Oh, Vi, I hope I haven't done the wrong thing by staying. At first, I turned down his invitation; he insisted I stay and I acquiesced."

"You didn't do the wrong thing. I am so glad you stayed; and Jim — surely, you can tell how happy he is that you didn't go home today!"

"Oh, I hope so. But enough about us. I want to know about you — especially about you and Dan. Is it alright for me to ask about him? If it is not, please tell me. I don't want to pry," Susan added.

"No, I'll gladly tell you about Dan. I think it will help me to finally talk about it with someone. I've just tried to handle my grief alone for all these months," Violet confessed.

Susan patted her hand and said sincerely, "I am so sorry for what you've gone through."

VIOLET began her story slowly, guardedly, and then moved into fast mode with her sad tale. "Dan and I have been sweethearts since High School. It seems I've loved him all my life. We always thought we would marry. When college choices were presented, we chose to go our separate ways, as painful as the separation would be. But our love for each other did not wane. In fact, it grew stronger with each passing year. So when we graduated last May, my graduation gift from Dan was an engagement ring. The wedding was scheduled for September. We had the date, the church, the flowers, and the attendants all lined up. Never had I been happier!

One weekend in June, a famous Christian speaker came to our church for a couple's conference. We had not planned to attend because we were so busy getting ready for the wedding. A dear friend of mine heard the guy speak on Friday night. She called me afterwards and said, 'Vi, you and Dan have to hear this guy! Why don't you plan to come tomorrow night?'

We really weren't that interested; but we decided, for her sake, we should go. What the speaker said that night changed everything for us. His message was on 'oneness' in marriage. He pointed out that a couple could not have true oneness if they were 'unequally yoked.' At that moment, I promise you, for the first time in all those years, a knot formed in my stomach. It was like a voice said to me, 'Do you know for certain Dan is a Christian? Do you know for certain that he has received Jesus Christ as his personal Savior and Lord? Does he want the same kind of marriage you want — built on Jesus Christ?' I was so upset I could hardly sit there. I wanted to have Dan answer those questions and of course, I wanted all the answers to be in the affirmative."

She continued: "As soon as the service was over, I told Dan I needed to leave. When we got to the car, he asked me what the problem was. I asked him to go somewhere where we could talk privately. He had no idea what was in my heart and mind. We went to our favorite little restaurant and sat in the back corner, where we had so often sat. He took my hands and looked into my eyes and said, "Baby, what in the world is so urgent?"

"Oh Dan," I declared, almost in tears, "what that speaker said made me think about some things, and I really got upset. Do you realize that we have never talked about our marriage from a spiritual perspective? We love each other so much that I think we just assumed that part would work out. But the speaker said that marriage was a three-part agreement — physical, mental, and spiritual. He said the marriage would be incomplete if in any of those ways a couple was not united and in one accord. I am positive you and I will not have a problem physically. Mentally, we think alike on social issues, on the family, and on values. But what about spiritually? Are we in one accord there?"

Then I hurriedly continued, "Dan, this past year, as you know, I've gotten closer to Jesus than at any time in my life. He is very real to me. I want Jesus Christ to be at the center of our marriage. Do you, Dan? Darling, is that what you want, too?" I asked in all earnestness.

"Dan stood up and came around to me. He put his hands on my shoulders and leaned over and kissed me on the forehead. 'Oh, Vi, of course I want this. What in the world would make you think I don't?' Then he knelt down beside me and took my hands in his. 'My precious Vi. No two people could love each other more than we do. Don't you know we are on the same wavelength and want the same things? We've dated for six years. We know almost everything about each other. Don't you think you can trust me to be to you what you need in this area? I love you more than life itself. I would do anything for you. You know that I want our marriage to be exactly what God wants it to be. Please don't let this speaker upset you.' Then he pulled my face toward him and kissed me.

"I was so touched by his words and his sincerity, I could not say anything else. He loved me so much, and I loved him with all my heart. At that moment I decided my questions were foolish. I felt I was not trusting him or trusting the Lord. I told him I was sorry I brought all this up — that I was just acting foolishly. We left the restaurant, came back here, and had a wonderful time. Susan, I never slept with Dan. It was something I simply was not going to do. Sex was to be saved for marriage, even if that idea seemed prudish and from the fifties. And Dan always respected me on that issue."

"Several days passed without my thinking much about what the speaker said. Then one morning when I was on my knees having my quiet time, I read Psalm 127:1 which says: 'Unless the Lord builds the house, They labor in vain who build it.'† I couldn't understand why that verse jumped out at me. I tried to put it out of my mind. I finished my quiet time and got up to get dressed. Then I flipped on the radio and a preacher was preaching on being 'unequally yoked with unbelievers.' I turned it off. My stomach was churning. I cried out to the Lord, *What is going on, Lord? I'm getting upset again. Dan loves me and I love him. You've never shown me any reason I shouldn't be marrying him."*

"But in that moment, the Holy Spirit impressed me to pray. I fell to my knees and cried out to my Heavenly Father: 'Lord, if this is not Your will, please stop me. I must not enter into a marriage that is not Your will, even though it would break our hearts into pieces that I'm not sure can ever be mended. But I surrender to Your will, Oh, dearest Lord. Please help me. I can't do this on my own.'"

"I remember that just then the phone rang. It was Dan. He sounded different. His voice was trembling. 'Vi, what have you been praying?' Dan asked me. 'My friend John Spritz just called me. He is that fanatic that was always preaching to everyone in our fraternity. You won't believe what he asked me.'

"What did he ask?" I inquired, beginning to tremble.

'He asked me if I had made things right with the Lord yet. I could not believe he was saying that. He used to say things like that all the time. I got to thinking about why he would call me now and ask me that. The only thing I could think was that maybe you were praying I would have an epiphany or something. Were you?'

'No,' I answered truthfully. 'I didn't pray for anything like that because I didn't think you needed an epiphany. Do you think you need an epiphany, honey?'

'I don't think so,' Dan answered. 'I think I'm doing just fine. Well, I'm running late. I'll talk to you later. I love you, baby. I love you so much. I love you more every minute. I can hardly wait until September.' He hung up the phone."

"I stood with the phone in my hand and stared at it. First the verse about the Lord building one's house; then the preacher preaching about 'being unequally yoked' Now, Dan had called and told me something I would never have believed."

"Oh, Susan," Vi declared as she stood up. "From that moment forward, every time Dan and I were together, there was tension. We didn't talk about this conversation again for weeks. Finally, one night I broke down and started crying. Dan was holding me in his arms on my sofa there in the living room. I pulled back from him and looked deeply into his eyes: 'Dan,' I said, 'my beloved future husband, I love you more than life itself. But I have to know. Have you had a personal encounter with Jesus Christ?'"

"Dan's face turned ashen. Then it got red and went from red to redder, as he just stared at me. Finally, he pulled away from me and stood up. He looked at me in a way I had never seen him look — he was filled with unbelievable anger. As I reached out to him, he turned, walked to the door and said: 'I love you, Vi. You know that. But you have pushed me to the limit. I will not be bullied on this issue! You and John Spritz can think what you want. But I'm not going to stay around to hear your accusations and questioning. I can't be married to a woman who doesn't trust me and doesn't think I'm good enough for her. It's over, Vi. It's over!' He stomped out the door, slamming it behind him."

"I was stunned and totally devastated. I could not believe this was really happening. Dan had walked out on me! After all these years we had been so in love, he does the unthinkable! He brings our relationship to an abrupt halt this way! I could not believe he had done this to me! He didn't ask for the ring back, but he might as well have done so. As the tears began to flow, I asked myself, *Is this all my fault or is this God's hand at work in Dan's life?*

For days I cried. I called Dan's phone again and again. I e-mailed him. I went by his office and his apartment. He would not see me, so I stopped contacting him. I sent the ring back by Jim with a note attached telling Dan that I loved him and wanted to marry him, etc. When Jim gave the ring and note to Dan, he admitted to Jim that his heart was broken, and he didn't know how he was going to live without me. But he could not go forward under these circumstances."

"So, Susan, that's the story. That was two months ago. Nothing has changed since that night he walked out of this house. All I can think is that Dan isn't a true believer, and he could not face that fact. I surrendered to God's perfect will for me; I have to trust that *this* is His will. If God wants us back together, He will have to do it, not me. My heart is broken! Sometimes I can hardly make it through the day because I miss him so much."

Susan got up and hugged Violet. She then said, "Oh, Vi, I am so sorry things have turned out like this. But I am so proud of you. You have done the right thing, cost what it may. Thank you for sharing your story with me. I will carry it with me always, as a beautiful and wonderful testimony of what total surrender to God's will really means. I just know in my heart that everything is going to work out eventually. Don't ever give up! I am certainly going to pray for you and Dan."

Suddenly Susan looked at her watch and exclaimed, "Oh, dear me, I have to get a shower and get dressed. Jim will be back and I won't be ready. Thanks for letting me stay here with you!" Susan gathered up her shopping bags and boxes and hurried to the guest room. Her heart was beating rapidly. As she walked to her room, her mind was racing. She began to compare her relationship with Jim to Violet's and Dan's. She silently thought: *Is our relationship a similar circumstance? Am I marching toward an abyss? Will our relationship fall apart like Dan's and Vi's?*

She could not let her mind dwell on those questions. Instead she said to herself: *I must pull myself together and focus on these wonderful hours I have to spend with Jim. Nothing must come between us that will spoil this weekend.* Suddenly she thought about Scarlet O'Hara in *Gone with the Wind*. Aloud she softly spoke: "I'll think about all this next week!"

CHAPTER SIXTEEN
CHAPTER SIXTEEN

AN hour later, as Susan walked down the hall toward the living room, she heard Jim talking with Violet. She started to open the door, but the words he was saying stopped her: "Oh, Vi, can you believe Susan? Can you believe how this has all worked out? All my life I've looked for the girl I wanted to marry. I honestly had given up. I did not think I would ever find anyone I truly wanted to spend the rest of my life with. I wanted a marriage like mom and dad's. But I didn't think there were marriages like that anymore. That is, until Susan Strasbourg came into my life. She is everything I've ever dreamed of and much, much more. I don't deserve her, but I love her more than I've ever loved anyone outside my family. Do you think she will marry me in spite of my faults and my wild side? She is so pure and good like you."

"Yes, Jim, I think she will marry you. I believe she really loves you. I do think you should be completely honest with her, though, about your bachelor years. She needs to know the good things and the not so good if she is going to be your wife. Don't expect a girl like her to go into marriage clueless and then just gloss over it when she hears about one of your escapades from an old friend of yours. Tell her the truth. Be open and honest with her. If she does love you, as I think she does, all that won't matter, I promise you," Violet concluded.

Once again fear crept into Susan's heart. *What on earth is she referring to? Oh, my goodness, I can't believe what she just said! But surely it can't be as bad as it sounds! I know Jim will tell me anything I need to know ... I've really got to go in there.* She took a deep breath and called out as she opened the door, "I'm finally ready. Were you about to give up on me, Jim?"

"Never, Sus, never." Jim replied. "Look at you in your new outfit. Doesn't she look great, Vi." Violet agreed. Jim took her hand and encouraged Violet to get her things and go with them. At first Violet turned him down. Then at Susan's urging, she agreed.

They went to Jim's favorite restaurant to eat. He suggested the shrimp salad, which Susan discovered was delicious. They had a great time with banter and teasing. The time seemed to be passing too quickly. Susan momentarily forgot the conversation she had overheard at Violet's house. She was enjoying the thrill of being here with Jim and Violet Hitchenson. *Can this be happening to me? Did I really hear Jim say that he wanted to spend the rest of his life with me?*

It was one thing for Jim to declare his love to *her*. For him to so passionately declare his love for her to his *sister*, the person he was closest to in the whole world, was thrilling and mind-boggling. Susan could hardly contain her joy. She wanted to jump and leap and praise God! Wisely, she used restraint. As they got up from their table, Violet headed in the direction of the ladies' room. Susan and Jim exited the restaurant and walked down the hill toward the marina.

THE sky was as blue as Jim had ever seen it. The blue-green water sparkled in the sunshine. The scattered white clouds that dotted the heavens made it a picture perfect day. His yacht stood like a small white castle in a beautiful fairy land. In Jim's heart was a feeling he had never had before — he was truly in love — and it was the greatest time of his life. But he wasn't just 'in love.' It was *who* he was in love with. He was in love with the most 'perfect' girl he had ever met — the purest, finest, most compassionate and caring woman — the most beautiful girl he had ever laid eyes on. It was almost too good to be true. His arm was around her, but he tightened his grip and pulled her as close to him as he could. He whispered in her ear, "Do you know who the happiest man in Georgia is, this beautiful afternoon?"

"No, who is he?" Susan teased.

"James Martin Hitchenson, Jr." He kissed her soundly on the lips.

When she recovered, Susan remarked, "That's the first time I've known your middle name, Mr. Hitchenson. Who were the Martins?" Susan asked.

My grandmother was a Martin. She named my daddy for her daddy, James Martin. My mother carried on the tradition. I am J. M. Hitchenson, Jr. What do you think?"

"I like it. May I call you 'Marty?' she inquired.

"No ma'am. You may call me 'Mr. Hitchenson.'" Jim teased back.

"I'll do it, kind sir."

Jim stopped abruptly. "I don't know *your* middle name."

Susan laughed. "No, I guess you don't. It's 'Olivia.'"

"You are kidding. That was my grandmother's name. I guess we'll have to name one of our daughters Olivia," he laughed and hugged her to his chest.

"You better stop that or someone might see us." Susan chided him lovingly.

"I hope they do, my love. I want the whole world to know that I love you!" Jim replied.

"Oh, Mr. Hitchenson, it's a beautiful, beautiful day." Susan whispered. Violet soon caught up with them and joined their walk to Jim's yacht.

On the way, they passed Dan's boat slip. Jim noticed his boat was gone. Out loud he spoke: "Dan must have his boat in the shop. I can't imagine he has taken it out this early on a Friday afternoon." Violet didn't say anything in response. She just looked over at the empty space. As they rounded the corner on the way to Jim's boat, they saw Dan coming up the waterway in his boat, heading toward his boat slip. Violet's expression changed immediately.

Jim called out to Dan. "Hi, Dan. Where have you been?"

"I decided to take a boat ride before everyone hit the water. It's really nice this afternoon. Who is that with you?" Dan asked.

"I have my sister, whom I believe you know, and my new girlfriend, Susan."

Dan smiled and was very friendly; but Violet turned her head away from him and kept walking forward, visibly upset. In a moment Dan spoke to Jim again: "Would you please tell your sister that I really need to talk with her. I've got something important to tell her that I think she will be very happy to hear."

"Yea, I'll tell her," Jim responded with a twinkle in his eye.

Dan added, "Why don't you tell her to meet me at my boat slip? Of course, if she is not interested in what I have to tell her, she doesn't have to come. See ya," Dan turned his attention back to his steering, as if it made no difference whether Violet came or not. That, of course, was the opposite of the truth. His heart had nearly jumped out of his body when he saw her. He knew this would be the time to reveal to her what had happened in his life recently. Even if she didn't respond as he wished, the news still needed to be told. She must know what Christ had done in his life!

Violet made a face. "I don't know whether to go back to Dan's boat or not. What in the world does he have to tell me?"

Jim noticed she was trembling. "I don't know, Sis. But if I were you, I'd give it a shot. He would not have said something if it wasn't important. After all, he was the one who broke up with you." Jim reminded her.

Vi answered: "I know, Jim. But do I really want to be that vulnerable? I don't think I can take much more." She sighed loudly. "What do you think I should do, Susan?"

"I think you should go. If you don't, you will always wonder what he wanted to tell you," was Susan's advice.

"You are both right. Okay. Please pray for me, Susan. I guess it's important that I know what he wants to tell me," Violet said as she turned around and headed in Dan's direction. When she was a few feet from his boat, her steps slowed. She stopped a moment to wipe the tears from her eyes, and then she continued her journey.

By this time Susan and Jim had reached his yacht. Jim pushed the button on his gadget and they walked onto the deck "It's even more beautiful in the daytime than it was at night," Susan remarked aloud.

"What is your favorite spot on this boat?"

"From now on, it will be wherever I am with you, my love. And I am very serious. These are not just words," Jim stopped and looked at Susan. "I want you here with me all the time! Don't ever forget that." They once again toured the beautiful yacht, ending up on the top deck, Susan's current favorite spot.

Dan looked up and smiled when Violet got within earshot. He called to her as she came near. "I'm a little surprised to see you. I didn't know if you would come or not. But I wanted to talk to you so badly, I just had to ask. I had been looking for an opportunity before today, but none had come."

Dan saw that she was not smiling or acting friendly toward him in any way. She had a somber look on her face. He didn't blame her. He knew her heart was broken, as was his.

"I came reluctantly," Violet admitted. She took a step, looked down at her feet and added, "But like Susan said, I would always wonder what you wanted to tell me if I didn't come." After what seemed like an eternity, she looked straight at Dan and bluntly asked, "Why *did* you want to talk to me, Dan?"

"Where do I begin?" Dan mused. "Can we go inside my boat and sit a minute?"

"I … I guess so," Violet answered. Dan could tell she was not anxious to grant his wish when she walked down the steps to the cabin.

"Why don't you sit over there and I'll sit here," Dan suggested. He was very nervous, but at the same time, excited.

Dan cleared his throat, moved to the edge of the chair and looked right into Violet's eyes: "First of all, Vi, I want to ask your forgiveness for running away from you and from the truth. You were right to ask those questions you asked me. John was right to ask his questions. But I'm a guy who has a lot of pride. I didn't want anyone accusing me of not being a true Christian. So I fought it and didn't want to face it. I know I hurt you more than I can possibly know. I know your heart has been broken.

You need to know that my heart was broken, too; but I was too proud to come back. When a certain young lady whom I love more than life itself, asked me those questions, questions I knew I could not answer, I tried to avoid the discussion. Then I chose the worst possible course — I ran away. Can you ever forgive me, my precious Vi," Dan asked, his eyes begging her forgiveness.

"Yes, I forgive you, Dan." She answered with a faint smile.

Quickly Dan spoke again, "Vi, those questions you asked kept nagging at me. The nagging in my soul wouldn't go away. I was miserable. I couldn't eat; I couldn't sleep. I worked out continuously. When I wasn't working out, I was taking the boat out and getting on my wave runner. When you would try to get in touch with me, I ran some more. That was not at all what I really wanted to do. I wanted to come running back to you and be reconciled; but I could not bring myself to do that."

"Then three weeks ago, something happened, Visie." Dan in one movement was kneeling at her feet. She reached for his hands and held them tightly in hers, gazing intently into his hazel eyes. He could hardly wait for her to hear his next words.

"A man came to town and spoke at an assembly at my alma mater, CBHS. I happened to be there for an alumni luncheon. Since I was early, I slipped into the back of the auditorium. I'm sure you would say it was not a coincidence. I thought it was at first. The speaker was talking about what mattered in life. He said a lot of things to the kids; then he went down on the floor with his mike and started walking back and forth. He told the kids that nothing mattered more than their relationship with Jesus Christ. He said, 'If you don't settle that now, no matter how successful you may be in life, you will not be a real success.'"

Dan stood up and walked back to the sofa and sat down again. Violet was now looking at him with a look he so clearly recognized — it was a look of love. It was difficult not to go over and embrace her, but he knew he must continue his story: "I'm not sure what all he said after that. I felt like he had been talking only to me. Did he know I was back there and that's why he said what he said? I didn't know; but at that moment I knew something in my life wasn't right and had to be taken care of. I felt like I would die if I didn't do something. I waited until the line of boys who wanted to speak to him had dwindled; then I started walking toward the front. He slipped away from the boys and started walking toward me. He reached out to shake my hand and said, 'Hello, Dan. You don't remember me, do you? I'm Rob Hansen, Class of 85.'

I was shocked, Visie. I had not heard him being introduced and I did not recognize him. He had shaved his head and put on some weight since high school." Violet smiled at his comment.

"I said, 'Hello, Rob. I'm sorry. I didn't recognize you. Good to see you.'

'It's good to see you, too, Dan. How have you been?' We exchanged pleasantries and then I heard myself asking if we could go somewhere to talk. He agreed, and we found an empty room. I began to tell him about our breakup as if he were a counselor. For me, that's what he was that day. After I had spilled my guts, he took a deep breath and said, 'Dan, I know God brought you here today. I prayed that someone would be here who needed change in his life. What you need is very simple. You need to receive Jesus Christ as your Savior and Lord. You haven't ever done that, have you?'

I sputtered and stammered and tried to convince him that I had done all the right things. 'I'm a good person and I've really tried to follow the Ten Commandments,' I finally told him. He wasn't impressed.

By this time, Dan was leaning forward and Violet had a huge smile on her face. She told him later she could hardly stay in her chair. "What happened next?" she eagerly asked Dan.

"I bet you know what I'm about to tell you. We got on our knees and I asked Jesus Christ to come into my heart and take over my life. I had that epiphany you wanted me to have!"

By this time Violet was in his lap, hugging him. "Oh, Dan, Oh, Dan, Oh, Dan." She kissed him with all the passion of her soul.

When the kiss had ended, Dan declared, "I love you, Visie, more than ever in my whole life. You were right all along. Can you forgive me for being so stubborn?"

Dan took her face in his hands and began to kiss her repeatedly. In the midst of this show of affection, she found a place to say, "Of course, my darling. I love you, Dan Holcombe; I always have and I always will!" For the next few minutes there was a tear-filled emotional reunion — a union of hearts such as neither one had ever experienced. Finally, Violet sat back in Dan's arms, smothered in his love as he gently stroked her hair and her cheeks.

"Marry me, Violet Hitchenson. Marry me today, tomorrow or next week. But let's not wait any longer. I do not want to live without you, my precious Vi, my only love."

Violet pulled away a little and replied, "I would be honored Mr. Holcombe. But may I have two weeks? I think it will take me that long to get everything together."

"If you must, baby, but no longer than that." Dan responded, as he held her against his chest. "I don't ever want to be away from you again. I promise never to leave you. Do you believe me?"

"I do. I do. I do … I'm practicing for the wedding," and they both laughed. "Should we let Jim and Susan know what's happened?" Violet finally asked.

"If you think we should," Dan responded. "I kind of like it right here. I could stay like this forever."

"I can't believe I jumped into your lap, Dan! I didn't even know what I was doing. It was just spontaneous. I was so excited, I could not hold back!" Violet exclaimed.

"You were exactly where you were supposed to be. It was the most natural and the most awesome thing in the world. It was a perfect fit — one we've experienced all these years."

"Oh, Dan," Violet exclaimed. "Do you have any idea how happy I am?"

"I think I do by knowing how happy I am. Love of my life, you are mine and I am yours, always and forever."

"Always and forever." Vi agreed, as she put her head on

Dan's shoulder. This is the only place I ever want to be — with you, my love, my life, my other half. I am yours, Dan, and only yours — forever and ever and ever … Amen."

Neither had any idea how much time had passed since Violet first came to the boat. Eventually they decided it was time to go and tell Jim and Susan what had happened. First, though, Dan wanted to know about Susan and what was happening with her and Jim. He was thrilled at what Violet told him. At the moment, he was too excited about his own situation to think about any future problems that might occur for Jim and Susan.

When they had climbed out of Dan's boat, Violet and Dan raced to Jim's yacht. They walked across the walkway and rang the doorbell. Jim called down from the upper deck. He pushed a button to unlock the door. Violet and Dan hurried up the stairs to where they were. Both Violet and Dan wanted to tell the story. Violet deferred to Dan. After all, it was his story, and it needed to come from him. When he had finished, Susan and Jim hugged them both. It was an exciting time! Violet and Dan would be getting married after all!

'Happy days were here again' for the Hitchenson family. Jim had found his true love; Violet and Dan had reconciled. At this moment in time, all was well. The rest of the day was full of excitement and jovial conversation. To celebrate, the foursome decided to go to Bombay, a favorite restaurant. Dan found himself immediately liking Susan. Jim was happy about that. The four of them were very congenial. They had a wonderful evening together.

Vicki,

Here is a copy of my new novel. Its target audience is

older teenage girls and single young adult women. I thought

you might want to read it; then please feel free to give it to

someone who might need to read it. I am especially asking mothers

and grandmothers of teenagers and young adults to share it with

daughters and granddaughters.

Love, Sarah O.

CHAPTER SEVENTEEN

CHAPTER SEVENTEEN

THE weekend was proceeding much too quickly for Susan and Jim. On Saturday they took the 'big boat' out and anchored it in Jim's favorite spot, Old Gray Cove. They jet skied and swam most of the afternoon. All too soon it was time to leave the water. When they had climbed back onto Jim's yacht, they headed toward the kitchen to get bottles of water. Susan touched Jim on the shoulder and said, "Jim, I need to tell you something." She began smiling.

He stopped and turned back to look at her. When he saw her smile, he relaxed. "What is it, baby?" he inquired, placing his hands on her shoulders. His look of love and caring could not have been mistaken. He loved this woman with all his heart; whatever she wanted to tell him was important and he wanted to hear what she had to say.

"I just don't think I can wait any longer to tell you this. Jim, I don't just *like* you a lot, I've fallen in *love* with you! I love you, Jim Hitchenson!" she emphatically told him as she moved her lips to his.

He barely got the words in, "Oh, baby," before they were expressing their mutual feelings for each other. They kissed for a long time. Then Jim pulled back and looked lovingly into those beautiful brown eyes, framed by sweeping dark brown lashes: "Susan, you have just made me the happiest man in the world. To know that the girl I love more than anything loves me, too, is almost unbelievable. I love you, my darling, Susan. If only I could tell you how much!"

The next few moments two very happy young people reveled in the joy of being in love. Too soon the reverie ended, and it was time to prepare for the arrival of their guests. Jim had invited Hal and Pat Kearney for dinner and a card game or two. Most of all, he wanted them to meet and get to know Susan. Hal and Pat Kearney were two of Jim's dearest friends. Their boat was anchored in Old Gray Cove beside Hitchens II.

The dinner was delicious and the card games lively and fun. The Kearney's stayed longer than they intended. All in all it was a great night! Just before they climbed out of Jim's boat and into theirs, Hal pulled Jim aside and said, "Jim, Susan is all you said she was and more. She is different from any of your girlfriends we have met. She has 'class,' and is not the typical girl out to catch a man. She's a keeper, Jim. Don't let her get away!"

"I don't intend to," was Jim's clear reply. "I plan to marry her … .if she'll have me."

At the same time, Pat was having her last good-byes with Susan. "Susan, dear, I hope with all my heart this won't be the last time we see you. I am so pleased we got to be with you tonight. You are surely one in a million! Give Jim a chance to prove himself. He has been looking for someone like you for a very long time. He needs you, Susan. You will be the 'making' of Jim Hitchenson." She left Susan dumbfounded and speechless.

Jim signaled his boat captain to lift anchor and head for the marina. Jim and Susan began to clean up everywhere. In the middle of the living room, Jim stopped and took Susan into his arms. He held her up off the floor and twirled her around. As they both giggled, he declared loudly, "I love you, Susan Strasbourg. And my friends loved you, too. Thank you for being such a wonderful hostess."

"That was not difficult with such nice folks. I really liked them, Jim. Pat and I hit it off right away. She is a doll."

"We'll see them often," Jim stated very matter-of-factly. They have stuck by me year after year. I've known them since I was a little boy. They have a great marriage!"

"That's wonderful to hear! They just seem like they would be 'true blue,' as my daddy used to say." Susan responded.

"Your daddy had lots of sayings, didn't he? I can hardly wait to meet him. He has to be one great guy! Anyone who likes boats and water has got to be someone I will like!" Jim added, grinning from ear to ear.

"You two will get along well," Susan added. "You are a lot alike. That's one reason I was attracted to you … Maybe I shouldn't have told you that … Is that okay?"

Jim laughed. "Of course, it's okay. Now, I am really anxious to meet him!" He hugged her and kissed her again. When he released her from his embrace, he started to say something, and then stopped.

She looked at him quizzically: "Jim, what are you thinking?"

"Oh, I was just thinking how nice it would be if you did *not* have to leave!" and he grinned a big, broad grin.

"I bet you were, Jim Hitchenson. But you might as well not 'go there.' I am going to Violet's, and the sooner, the better." She grinned at him as she gathered her things.

The yacht was approaching the marina. An awesome day was almost over. Not wanting to go ashore, Jim reluctantly helped her disembark from his yacht. They carried some things to Jim's car.

Violet's house was about thirty minutes away. When they got to Violet's, Dan was still there. Not wanting to intrude, Jim suggested they go around to the back door. He unlocked it, calling out to Violet as they entered; he didn't want her to think it was a prowler. "We're home, Vi and Dan. We'll be back here in the kitchen for a while." Jim continued.

Immediately Violet and Dan came to the kitchen. Dan spoke first: "Hi folks. How was it on that little boat of yours?" He laughed as he spoke and pulled Violet to his side. "It could not have been better than it was right here!" and he kissed Violet without any embarrassment.

"Now, Dan, baby, you will embarrass Susan." Violet verbalized.

"Don't think so," Dan answered. "Don't care, either!"

"Dan Holcombe, now you're embarrassing me!" The teasing and banter continued as they talked about the events of the day. It would go down as one very memorable day for both couples.

CHAPTER EIGHTEEN
CHAPTER EIGHTEEN

ON Sunday morning they awoke to rain and fog. It would have been easy to turn over and go back to sleep. There wasn't enough time to eat breakfast. Coffee had to do this morning! Even though they hadn't slept much, all four would make it to church on time.

Susan wore her blue suit she wore the night Jim first saw her. His heart leaped as she walked down the hall toward him. He exclaimed loudly, "My favorite outfit!" Then he whispered in her ear, "Until our wedding day, it will remain my favorite!"

Violet and Dan had gotten to the church before them and saved seats. Mr. and Mrs. Hitchenson were seated on the other side of Violet and Dan. Susan smiled and spoke to them as she and Jim were being seated. They returned the greeting warmly with smiles and hello's. Susan felt so secure sitting there with Jim's entire family. He took her hand and placed it on his knee. Surely, she must be in Heaven!

After the service, many people were coming up to greet them. It seemed the entire church was focusing on the Hitchenson's this morning. By this time the news had spread: Jim has a *real* girlfriend and Dan and Violet are back together. Everyone appeared to be thrilled!

Hal came up to speak to Jim and Susan, but a girl whom Susan did not know had gotten Susan's attention. She called her from the other end of the row: "Susan, I'm Victoria Smithson." Susan moved toward her. She was now away from earshot of everyone else.

"I have heard that you and Jim are dating. I just want to warn you, my dear. Jim Hitchenson is not a 'one woman man.' He will tell you he loves you while he's saying the same thing to someone else. He cannot be trusted. You need to know that."

Susan was turning white as a sheet. She was flabbergasted! She had no idea how to respond to these accusations. Finally, she softly replied, "Victoria, I know you mean well, but you need to know that I trust Jim to be a man of his word," and she turned and walked back to where Jim was standing. She touched his arm and whispered that she needed to leave immediately.

Jim excused himself from Hal and they took off down the aisle without stopping to talk to anyone else. He saw that Susan was visibly upset and he wanted to know why.

"Susan, tell me, what happened in there?" He asked as they hurriedly headed toward Jim's Porsche.

"Victoria really upset me, Jim," Susan replied as she turned so no one could see her face.

"Susan, you're crying. What in the world did she say?" Jim asked with great concern.

"Let's get in the car and I'll tell you," Susan answered.

When both were seated in the car, Jim started the engine in order for the air conditioning to cool down the hot car. He then turned and faced Susan. Susan blurted out, "Victoria told me she wanted to warn me about you, Jim. She told me not to trust you!"

Jim stiffened and interrupted her, "I can't believe she would say something like that to you!" His face showed his rising anger. "What right did she have to upset you like that? I haven't seen or talked with her in years." He sat back in his seat, with an amazed look on his face.

"Let's see. I dated her twice and that was all. I was told she was in love with me, but I was never interested in her. She tried to get me to go to bed with her, but for once, I did not. Maybe she has a grudge against me … I can't believe she did this … " He stopped and looked off and then turned back to Susan, taking her hands in his. "Oh, Sus, I am so sorry about this." He leaned forward. "Baby, I'm so very, very sorry. What can I do?"

"It's okay, Jim, I didn't believe her," Susan said sadly. She released one of her hands to pat him gently on the arm.

Everything was silent for a few minutes. Jim backed the car out of its parking place. They rode along holding hands and thinking to themselves. Then Susan broke the silence. "I guess I should tell you exactly what she said. I don't think we ought to hold anything back from each other. I believe in being open and forthright, don't you?"

"Absolutely. I want to know everything. Was there something else?" Jim asked in disbelief.

"She told me that you were not a 'one woman man.' That you might be telling one girl you loved her, but at the same time telling another girl the same thing. That's when she warned me not to trust you." Susan had spilled it all out. The tears were creeping onto her cheeks by that time. She got out a Kleenex and began to wipe away her tears.

Jim made a sharp turn into an empty bank parking lot, and put the car into Park. He shifted in his seat so he could look fully into Susan's tearful brown eyes. As she gazed at his troubled face, he reached out and put his hands on her shoulders.

"Oh, Susan, don't you know with us there is nothing that could be further from the truth?! In the first place, I have never told two girls that I loved them both. I have done some things I'm not proud of, where women are concerned. But that is not one of them. I want you to know that. And where you and I are concerned, I have never loved anyone like I love you. There is no one else in my life but you. Besides that, I don't intend for there to ever be anyone in my life but you. You may not want it to be that way, but I do with everything that is in me. I love you, Susan, and you alone. The love I have for you is unlike any love I have ever known!" Jim took a breath and moved his hands to hers, but he wasn't through with his dissertation and declaration.

"Maybe you feel like you shouldn't trust me. I'm sure I haven't always been a trustworthy man; but I would never knowingly do anything to betray *your* trust. Do you believe me at all, Susan?" Jim pleaded.

Susan reached over and kissed Jim on the cheek before she answered him. "Oh, Jim. I do trust you. I do not think you are just saying that you love me. I know you love me. I can tell it by the way you've treated me these past few days — by the way you look at me — protect me — respect my wishes — by the way you kiss me. I've never had anyone treat me as you have — with love and respect and kindness and tenderness like I've never known. I did not believe her when she said it. I love you, Jim, and I know you love me. If it is God's will, our relationship will continue, and no one can stop it." Susan paused, rubbing Jim's arm.

"Oh Susan," Jim declared. "I love you more than I thought it was possible to love anyone! I want to spend the rest of my life proving my love to you."

Suddenly, Susan interrupted his 'dialogue of devotion' and exclaimed, "Jim, did you realize we are sitting in the middle of an empty bank parking lot in broad daylight? It's a wonder a crowd has not gathered! I think we better continue this conversation later. We're already late for lunch." Susan sat back in her seat and smiled. Jim agreed and started the engine. Soon there were turning into the Country Club.

When they walked into the dining room of the Club, Violet knew immediately something was wrong. Had Jim and Susan had their first lovers' quarrel? Something definitely had happened, and Violet had no idea what it was.

She turned to Dan and said, "Something is wrong with Jim. I wonder what has happened." At that moment she wondered if their relationship was too good to be true.

"I don't know what the problem could be, but we'll find out soon enough." Dan responded.

Jim and Susan sat down across from Violet and Dan. "Hello you two," Violet said smiling. "What took you so long?" she asked, half kidding.

"Oh, I couldn't get Jim away from all those admirers," Susan said kiddingly. "I finally dragged (or is it drug) him away."

"You better watch those girls at church, Susan. They are all out to get him."

"She discovered that, I can assure you." Jim interrupted abruptly, not smiling. "We have some real 'lulus' at our church."

So that's the problem, Violet thought to herself. *Someone at church said something that did not go well with one of the two or perhaps both.* Violet knew at that moment she should have warned Susan about what someone might say to her. After all, most of the girls she knew at church were dying for Jim to notice them. He hadn't, though — not a one of them. Today at lunch Violet probably would not find out what happened at church — but she would find out! She watched as Susan succeeded in getting Jim to settle down and participate in other conversations before they finished lunch.

The next stop was the Hitchenson mansion. By the time they reached his parents' home, Jim was more relaxed. He wanted Susan to see his family as well as his home. It seemed Susan and his family now had a 'mutual admiration society.' She had won a place in the family, even in this short time. When he thought about it, it was a very short time that any of them had known

Susan. What a difference a week makes!

Soon it was time to depart. Susan hugged Mr. and Mrs. Hitchenson good-bye. They made sure she would be at the wedding in two weeks. "We'll look forward to seeing you then," they told her. Their sincerity was unmistakable.

Jim took Susan by Violet's to get her things. She heard Dan ask when they would see each other again. Jim told him he was going to North Carolina to spend the next weekend with Susan. He would get there Friday in time to go by the office in Morganton. Jim hoped that would be good news to Susan.

As they arrived at the airport, Jim's demeanor was downcast. "I don't want you to go, Susan. I guess I'll always feel this way every time you leave me. Will you feel this way when I have to go on a trip?" asked Jim.

Susan wasn't sure how to respond. She mumbled, "Of course, I will." They both smiled.

Jim helped her with her bags and waited until she was checked in. Soon Susan would go through security. They stepped aside and he took her in his arms. "This has been the most unbelievable week of my life. I can't believe I have really found you — the girl of my dreams — the love of my life. Please take good care of yourself until I come. I will call you every day. You can call me any time. I love you, Susan Strasbourg. Don't ever forget that!"

"Oh, how could I, Jim? This has been the most wonderful week of my life – it's been a dream come true. Thank you for everything. Most of all, thank you for loving me. I love you, Jim. I can hardly wait till Friday. Call me."

Jim grabbed her and kissed her tenderly. He ignored the passersby completely. It was okay for all the world to know: Jim Hitchenson was through playing around; he was settling down with the most awesome woman in the world — the love of his life. He was one happy man. Tell the whole world, if you liked;

that would be fine with him.

Jim called her on her cell phone as Susan walked down the concourse to her gate. He wanted her to know that he already missed her. A few minutes later as she sat in the waiting area, he called her again. Since she had to cut the call short because it was time to board the plane, she assumed they would not talk again until she got home. As she settled in her seat on the plane, her phone rang again. Oh, this was fun! She loved it!

CHAPTER NINETEEN
CHAPTER NINETEEN

WHEN Susan was back in her condo in Morganton, she called Jim. "I'm home," she told him.

"No, you're not. Home is here with me. That's just where you are living right now," Jim teased. "It's your *temporary* dwelling,"

"Jim Hitchenson, you are a sight! Okay, I'm at my condo safe and sound. But I miss you terribly!"

"Not as much as I miss you, my Beautiful Prude. I shouldn't have let you go. We should have eloped this weekend … Why didn't I think of that?" Jim wondered aloud.

"I'm not much on eloping, Jim. I've always liked the idea of walking down a church aisle in a flowing white wedding gown!"

"That you will do, BP. But don't think you can wait much longer to fulfill your vision. It has got to come to pass very soon." Jim added.

"I'll give that some careful attention," Susan said.

"Real careful attention, my lady," Jim responded. "Real careful. Make it a high priority on your list of things to do this week. And remember, this comes from your boss — he always knows what is best for his employees. He is a rational man."

"Oh, yes, I know about that," Susan answered. "I will

certainly have to give this matter my greatest consideration, won't I?"

"Absolutely. I'll give you at least twenty-four hours to ponder it," Jim told her. "I'll call you tomorrow at this time to see what you are thinking."

"Jim Hitchenson, you are impossible! But I like you, nonetheless. I'm going to call it a night, now. Sweet dreams."

"Whoa, there, lady. I believe I heard you say you *liked* me; but I didn't hear the 'love' word. I don't think I can have sweet dreams if you just 'like' me."

"I love you, Jim Hitchenson," Susan responded lovingly. "There's no way I could tell you tonight how much. I wish you could come through this phone. It hurts so much to be separated from you. But just so you'll know ... I *like* you, too, my love."

By this time, Jim was 'dying' inside; but he was also elated at what he was hearing. "Oh, Susan, I love you with all my heart — I miss you so much I can hardly stand it. Come home, baby, come home soon."

"I will, Jim. I promise. Good night, my love."

"Good night, sweetheart." Jim responded.

Neither wanted to be the first to hang up. Finally, Jim heard the phone click. His 'woman' had gone back to North Carolina. For the first time reality hit him — Susan was gone. Sadness enveloped him. He began to ask himself: *Is this how it is when you love someone like I love Susan? Do you feel so lonely without her you think you're going to die and wish you would?!* He couldn't stand it, so he called Violet.

"Vi, honey, I know it's late, but I'm so lonely I could die. Is this normal? Is this the way you feel when Dan's not there with you?" Jim asked his sister.

"Oh, yes, Jim, it is. I can hardly stand to be apart from him. I don't know how I'm going to wait a few more days to marry him!" Violet answered.

"Vi, I didn't know what I had been missing. Why didn't you tell me to quit 'playing around' and look for my wife?" Jim pleaded.

"Because that would not have worked. Your future wife had to come into your life before you would be willing to give up messing around. You had to meet this girl and fall in love with her. Then you would realize what you had been missing — then and only then … .Oh, Jim, I am so excited about Susan. She is wonderful and just perfect for you. I believe she really loves you, Jim. She is going to make a wonderful wife and mother, don't you agree!?" Violet asked.

"I more than agree, Sis. I can hardly wait! Being with her is not like anything I have ever known. Mother was right when she told us we would *know* when the right one came along. I knew almost immediately that Susan was *the one!*" Jim excitedly declared.

"Oh, Bro, I'm so happy. So very, very happy for you both … .When do you think you'll get married?" Violet asked.

"I don't know; but I told her tonight I wanted it to be as soon as possible," Jim responded.

MONDAY morning seemed to dawn earlier than usual. Susan had not realized how tired she was. It had been a fantastic week, but a draining one — emotionally and physically. Now, it was Monday morning; she was certain it would *feel* like Monday all day long.

At seven-thirty the phone rang. It was Jim. His call brightened things considerably. He was counting the days till

Friday and wanted her to know it. He told her, "I was just thinking this morning, that in a few weeks I won't have to call you to talk with you in the morning. You will be right there beside me when I wake up. I can hardly wait."

"Oh, Jim, I can't let myself think that way this morning. I'm gonna be late to work if we start talking that way. I don't think my boss will be happy if I'm late," she teased.

"You *are* the boss, honey. You don't have to get there on time," Jim responded.

"Oh, but I have to set a good example. When you've just won an award for your performance, that probably is not a good time to falter, do you think?" Susan queried him.

"You win this time, but not for long. Soon you won't have to get up early on any Monday morning, as far as I am concerned. By the way, before you go, I have something I need to tell you. I love you, Susan Strasbourg; and I always will." Jim emphasized at the end.

"I love you, Jim Hitchenson; and I always will. Have a great day, my love ..."

"I love you, sweetheart. Manager of the Year. The future Mrs. Hitchenson. Have a fantastic day!" He reluctantly let her go. Oh, how he longed to gaze into her eyes and hold her in his arms once more; but he could only dream about it at this moment, because she was in North Carolina and he was in Atlanta.

Then he had an idea. *I'll send her roses today. Lots and lots of roses.* Like the movie, *Bed of Roses*, he would surround her with roses. Didn't the rose symbolize love? Sure it did; and he would shower her with his love by sending bouquets of roses. He called the florist. "I want you to send roses to this address — he had to look it up on his computer — every hour on the hour today from nine until four. Send red and pink and coral and yellow with red edges — just the most beautiful roses you can find," he told the florist.

So they started coming. Roses and more roses. Then more roses. American Beauty Roses, pink roses, lavender roses, coral roses. There were yellow roses with red edges — her very favorite. She and her staff were overwhelmed. When the first roses arrived, she tried to call Jim to thank him; his phone went immediately to call waiting. She placed the first two bouquets on her desk. When the third and fourth dozen appeared, she started giving a bouquet to each lady in her office.

About two o'clock she called and left him a voice mail: "Jim, the roses are wonderful! I love them all! They are beautiful, and you were wonderful to send them. But don't you think it's time to stop the deliveries? I don't have any place left to display them. I love you, Jim. What a beautiful, beautiful Monday I've had, thanks to you." At that moment a call was coming in on her phone. She clicked on the 'answer' window. It was Jim.

He told her excitedly, "I've avoided talking to you in person today because I didn't want to spoil the surprise. I couldn't stand it any longer. I love you, Mrs. Hitchenson- to- be. And I'm glad you and the girls in the office like the roses. But I wish I could have sent myself, instead. I have not accomplished anything today. All I could think about was you, Susan. Do you have any idea what you have done to me?" he inquired lovingly.

"I don't know, Jim. I just know what you've done to me. I can't think about anything but you and our time together. I know all this has really happened, but it seems too good to be true. Is this really Jim Hitchenson I'm talking to?" Susan asked playfully.

"Afraid so. The very same," answered Jim. "There are only two of us that I know about, and you are not talking to the elder one."

"Jim," Susan said after a few seconds. "Do you miss me as much as I miss you?"

"More, I'm sure. You couldn't possibly miss me as much as I miss you. I didn't know it could hurt so much to love someone like I love you and not be able to be with them. I don't think I can wait until Friday to come." Jim responded.

"Then don't, Mr. Hitchenson. Just come on down and inspect your Morganton office. You are welcome any time." Susan laughed, thinking how she wished he would come the next day.

Jim got a phone call which he had to take. "I've got to answer this call, my love. I'll talk to you later this afternoon. I love you." Then he was gone.

"I love you back, Jim." Susan answered, but Jim had gone. Suddenly, she felt so empty inside. *Is this what it's going to be like? Am I going to feel empty every time we have to hang up the phone, or leave each other's side? What a way to live! I'm not sure I can stand for it to be this way!*

CHAPTER TWENTY
CHAPTER TWENTY

BY Tuesday evening, Jim was calling Susan on a regular basis, both morning and night. When the phone rang on Tuesday night, Susan assumed it was he. She almost answered the phone, "Hello, my love." Something restrained her, and instead she just said, "Hello."

The voice on the other end was not a man's voice, however, but a woman's. She was surprised. "Susan, this is Pat Kearney. You know, we came to Jim's boat for dinner."

"Of course, Pat. I certainly know who you are. What a nice surprise to hear from you. How are you?" Susan asked.

"Oh, I'm fine, honey. I am in Asheville, and I was thinking about you and Jim. I wish I had called you earlier so you could have come over tonight. It's not very far from Morganton, is it?" Pat asked.

"No, it's not. Where are you staying?"

"I'm at the Grove Park Inn. We love it here." Pam responded.

"Oh, our family does, too. When Jim comes this week, we're going there and to the Biltmore. Believe it or not, Jim has never been to the Biltmore. How is Hal?" Susan asked.

"He is fine. He is not here with me; I'm here for a Garden Club Convention." Pat replied. Then she moved the conversation to the reason for her call.

"Susan, I want to talk to you about something. Is this a convenient time?" she inquired.

"Oh, yes. This time is perfect," Susan answered, eager to know why Pat was calling.

"Well, it's about Jim." She sighed and Susan's heart leaped into her throat.

"Is something wrong?" Susan responded. She was obviously worried.

"No, honey. Now, please don't let me upset you. I've called to assure you of something, not worry you. I've been talking with Jim the last few days. He has been so upset about what Victoria said to you at church. It made him very angry. He has been trying to figure out why she would say all that to you. That's why he called me. He wanted a woman's insight."

Susan said, "I see." Then she asked, "What did you tell him, Pat, if you don't mind my asking."

"Well, Susan, I've known Victoria for years. I think she has been in love with Jim all this time. Many years ago he made the mistake of taking her out twice. I believe the reason she told you that he was not a 'one woman man' was because she is so disillusioned — she thinks *she* is his 'other woman.' I don't think I have to tell you that is absolutely not true — she has never even been on his 'radar.' But I cannot think of any other reason she would say what she did to you. Jim is not a two-timer. He has never been. On the contrary, he really cannot stand two-timing. Through the years I have heard him say many times that two-timing is 'gross deceit.' I can assure you there is *no other woman* in his life!" Pat had emphasized the last statement. She wanted Susan to know the truth about Jim. Susan breathed a sigh of relief. Pat's call was a godsend.

"Oh, Pat, thank you so much for calling and for explaining this to me. It helps so much. And I know it helped Jim to talk with you. He was so upset with Victoria for saying what she did to me. It hurt him deeply. I tried to convince him that I didn't believe her — I even told *her* I didn't believe what she was saying. Yes, she warned me not to trust him; but I *do* trust him, Pat. I trust him completely. I know he loves me and me alone. I don't know how to explain it; I just know it."

Pat laughed. "Oh, honey. You are right on the money. Jim loves you like I never thought he could love anyone. He worships and adores you. His whole focus is on making you happy and on being the man he should be for you. You are right to trust him — He loves you with all his heart." They talked on for a few minutes. Then Pat said, "There's one more thing, Susan. You need to know that we have told Jim he needs to level with you about things from his past that might come up. You never know who else might say something to you. He has promised us he would. I told him that your love was strong enough to overcome anything he might tell you."

Then she added: "Jim is not a bad person, Susan. I've known him all my life. He is really a great guy — a gentleman through and through. He's a real 'people person.' He loves people. Yes, he will tell you he has made some poor choices along the way. He regrets them all. But he is a true blue friend — loyal to the core. We have been friends since we were in grade school. He has stood by his friends, in good times and in bad. We know him very well, and we love him dearly."

Pat continued: "Susan, I probably shouldn't tell you this — but Jim is afraid of losing you. I have never seen him like this. I told him that what I had seen in your eyes and heart made me believe that you had given your heart to him. I could not imagine anything that could cause you to break up with him."

Susan was quiet for a moment. Then she said, "Oh, Pat. There is not but one thing that could ever come between Jim and me; and that one thing is not a *thing*, but a *person*. The only Person who could ever get me to break up with Jim is God!"

Pat gasped on the other end of the line. "Did you say 'God'?" she asked in disbelief.

"Yes, I did." Susan answered emphatically. "I want only God's perfect will to be done in my life and Jim's. I believe God approves of this marriage. The only way it won't take place is if God tells me not to marry Jim. I pray earnestly that will not happen. I love Jim Hitchenson more than I ever thought it was possible to love anyone. I cannot imagine life without him."

There was an uncomfortable pause in their conversation. Pat was at a loss for words. She had never heard anyone talk this way. Her friends didn't talk about God. Religion was a subject that almost never came up in their discussions. Their relationships with God were private matters they kept to themselves. Here Susan had not only brought up the subject, but talked about it in a way Pat had never heard before. She recovered somewhat and said, "Well, Susan, that's great. I felt sure your response would be positive. I'm not sure I should have told you all this; but I felt like you would want to know. I'm sure everything is going to work out wonderfully well. You and Jim make the perfect couple, in my book. Good night, dear. So good to talk with you." Pat was finished. Susan thanked her for calling and told her good-bye.

As she hung up the phone, she felt the emotion of fear rising within her. Jim's past seemed to hover over their relationship like an evil specter. She determined not to let this fear have control of her — she would trust God in the midst of this turmoil. She silently claimed the verse in I John 4:4: "He who is in you is greater than he who is in the world." Turning on a Praise CD, she began singing praises to her Heavenly Father. Soon she was sound asleep.

CHAPTER TWENTY-ONE

CHAPTER TWENTY-ONE

SINCE Jim had called Susan day and night on Tuesday and Wednesday, when she did not get her wake-up call from him on Thursday morning, she was surprised and a little hurt. *Why did he not call?* Not allowing herself to fret about it, she dialed him up. His cell phone went to 'call waiting' immediately. *If he isn't at his office, where can he be? Enough of that*, she thought. *I must get dressed and get to work for my eight-thirty meeting!*

She made it to the office on time, and as planned, met with one of their clients. About ten-thirty, she heard some commotion in the front office. Just then her business phone rang. "Susan, there is someone up here who would like to have a word with you! Can you come to the front desk?" Her receptionist sounded so excited she could hardly speak. Was she happily excited or really upset about this person being there? Wondering what in the world was going on, Susan moved her work aside, got up from her chair and started to the front. It was then that she saw him! It was Jim! He had come a day early! Here he stood 'in living color' right before her eyes!

Susan didn't know whether to rush into his arms or shake hands with him. He was grinning as she approached where he was standing. He just grabbed her and hugged her like there was no tomorrow. She jumped back, embarrassed and exclaimed, "Mr. Hitchenson, we weren't expecting you until tomorrow. How nice of you to come a day early." Feeling like that was a dumb thing to say, she just stood there and grinned at him as he grinned back.

"I needed to come on today, Miss Strasbourg. I hope you don't mind," Jim replied. "I flew into the Asheville-Hendersonville airport, rented a car and came the short distance to Morganton."

Gathering her wits, she gently took his arm and said, "We are thrilled to have you here. Let me introduce you to everyone. By the way, you can see that your roses are still beautiful; they have added greatly to the decor of our office. We all want to thank you for this incredible gift." Several of the female employees eagerly agreed.

Susan guided Jim him around the office and introduced him to everyone. He was as gracious as she expected him to be. He took his time with each employee. He would sit on the employees' desks if there was room, and inquire of each how he or she came to work for Hitchenson Enterprises. Needless to say, he was a real 'hit' with the employees. After he had spent time individually with each one, he asked them all to come to the front lobby for a question and answer session. This informal gathering lasted about thirty minutes.

By this time it was noon. Jim ended his meeting with the employees by saying, "It has been great to meet all of you. Now, if you would please excuse Miss Strasbourg and me, we have some business to take care of. If you have questions at any time, please e-mail me. I always want to be available to each of you. You are doing a great work. And I know you are proud of your manager being named Manager of the Year for Hitchenson Enterprises. I know we were thrilled that she received the award!" He stood and concluded by saying, "It has been a pleasure to meet all of you. Miss Strasbourg, would you please escort me to your office."

Jim reached for Susan's hand and followed her to her office. The employees watched, goggle-eyed. He closed the door behind him and gazed into her eyes for a brief moment before he drew her into his arms. He kissed her again and again. "I have missed you so much, Sus. I couldn't wait until tomorrow to come," he said as they embraced once more. She laid her head on his shoulder. It felt so right.

Jim continued, "I wasn't accomplishing a thing at the office. I decided I could accomplish a lot more by being with you. Are you sure you don't mind?" Jim asked. "I love you, baby. I love you so much!"

Susan lovingly gazed into his eyes and exclaimed, "Oh, Jim, thank you, thank you for coming early. I don't think I could have made it till Friday! I love you, I love you, I love you."

"Let's get out of here!" Jim said abruptly, still grinning from ear to ear.

He opened the door as Susan gathered her things. As he walked with Susan past the employee's stations, he started speaking again, loudly enough for all to hear. "I am taking Miss Strasbourg to lunch. I don't think we'll make it back this afternoon. Tomorrow we go on a trip. You will excuse her, I'm sure. If you need her, you can call her cell phone. It has been great to be here in Morganton. God bless you all." He escorted Susan out the front door, leaving behind a startled, smiling group of people.

As they headed for their cars, she finally was able to speak, "Oh, Jim. What do you think they thought about that exit?"

"Don't know and don't care, my fair lady. You're here and I'm here; and that's exactly what I want!" Jim responded.

"You are something, Mr. Hitchenson. Wonder where I found you? ... And now that I've found you, do you think it is possible I can keep you?" Susan remarked.

Then she suddenly stopped, "Oh, my goodness! What am I saying? Where did that come from?" She was thoroughly embarrassed. When she had first met Jim she had told him she *liked* him a lot. Now, it sounded like she was proposing.

Jim jumped right in, delighted that she had blurted out her

true feelings. "Yes, ma'am, you can keep me; and not just for this weekend — you get to keep me forever! Thanks for asking. That's just what I planned to ask you!" Jim poked her in the side and laughed loudly. "Now, let's see you try to get out of that one, my Beautiful Prude. You have gotten yourself into an arrangement that you are not going to be able to get out of."

Susan didn't know what to say back to Jim. Her words had sounded much like a proposal. Why in the world did she say that to him, she wondered? Had she sounded like a blithering idiot? He didn't seem to think so; but she wished those words had not come out of her mouth. "Oh, Jim," she finally said. "I wasn't being serious, I was just kidding around."

In a little boy voice he pleaded: "Don't you want to keep me, Miss Strasbourg? Now that you've found me, are you going to throw me out? Oh, ma'am, please let me stay! I won't be too much trouble. You won't be sorry," and he took her by the arms and looked at her with a sad, child-like look.

She burst out laughing and replied, "No, Jim, I am not going to throw you away. You are the most wonderful treasure I have ever found. There is no way I intend to get rid of you.

"Finders, keepers. Losers, weepers."

"Well, that's a relief," Jim laughed and let go of her arms. He reached for one of her hands. He held out his free hand for her keys. She deposited them in his open hand. Jim pushed the unlock button on the keying tab and opened the door for her. Their plan was for her to pull her car around to his and let him follow her to the restaurant where they would have lunch. What a day this had already been for both of them! When she felt she had just goofed, Jim didn't seem to mind. The truth was he loved it. It would be something they would always look back on — he with glee, and she with embarrassment.

CHAPTER TWENTY-TWO

SUSAN had no idea how Jim planned to spend this long weekend with her. At the moment, she didn't care. Driving to the restaurant alone she prayed, "*Lord, please help me keep my wits about me. Please give me guidance, wisdom and strength. I claim the verse in Philippians 4:13 for these days with Jim: 'I can do all things through Christ who strengthens me.'† In Jesus' Name, Amen.*"

She pulled into the parking lot behind Gorbey's. Jim followed her and found a parking spot nearby. He got out of his car and walked toward her. When she stepped out of her car, she heard him ask: "Would you like to have lunch with me, dear lady?" He smiled that smile so familiar to her now. "I'm new in town and need someone to eat with me. It would be a pleasure to have you join me."

"Possibly, sir. But I don't believe I got your name." Susan played along.

"It's Martin. Martin Hitchens." Jim replied.

"Well, hello, Mr. Hitchens. I'm so happy to meet you. Is Martin a family name? I haven't met many men whose first name was 'Martin.'" Susan could not keep from laughing as she said it.

"Oh, yes. My grandmother was a Martin." Jim replied.

"Well, I like it. It's nice to meet you. Thank you for asking me to join you." Susan responded with a twinkle in her eye.

Their lunch time was joyful — filled with teasing and fun for them both. They relished being in each other's company. They were getting to know and like each other better and better. Their personalities were quickly gelling. Who would have thought it was only a week ago they met for the first time?

Susan took Jim to her apartment after lunch. Already dressed casually, he waited in the living room while she put on something more comfortable. They were going to tour Morganton, her home town. Morganton was a unique place nestled in the foothills of the Blue Ridge Mountains. The rolling hills made a lovely setting for the expansive tree-lined grounds of the famous hospital for the mentally ill. Several unique edifices were at the center of the campus, the most impressive of which was the main building, with its cupolas and towering dome. Built in the 1900's, it stood proudly as if to say, "Time has had no effect on me."

The tour of Morganton took them on one of the city's bypasses. A Greenway was bordered by the road. As they cleared the trees, the vista to the left of them included the School for the Deaf and the mental hospital. The latter overshadowed the former. As they passed the country club and tennis courts, Jim asked if Susan would like to play tennis later. The answer was "yes." First, she wanted to show him the house where she grew up, the schools she attended and the church her family loved so much. After that, they would head for Lake James. Jim wanted to rent a boat and spend much of the rest of the day exploring the beautiful lake.

"Should we rent a pontoon or a deck boat?" Jim asked Susan when they got to the lake marina.

"Perhaps a deck boat," Susan answered. "Then we could go fast or slow. I honestly don't think of you as a 'pontoon guy.'"

"You know that's right," Jim laughingly responded. "I never thought I'd own a slow boat. That is why I have two jet skis. They allow me to 'fly' across the water. For years I owned a really neat cigarette boat. You know how those boats can move!"

"Like something shot out of a cannon," Susan agreed. "One of those cigarette boats almost made our little boat capsize in the tremendous wake it left. Every time we saw one coming our way, we held on to the sides of our fishing boat. Daddy would usually have something to say about them being too fast to be on our part of the lake."

"I'm sure I upset a lot of folks those years I had that boat. I really tried to keep it in the middle of the lake. But sometimes I'm sure my speed was excessive. I guess they developed those boats for adventuresome men like me. It was a fun 'big boy toy' those years I owned one!" Jim added.

He paid for the deck boat, which happened to be in great condition, and they both climbed in! Jim started the engine and the boat moved slowly out of the slip. It felt so great to be on water again!

After riding in silence a few moments, Susan remarked, "This is a beautiful *blue* day, I think, Jim. The sky is blue, the water is blue, and the mountains are blue! I never thought about it that way before!" Susan laughed. Then she quickly added, "But the atmosphere is anything but blue! It is a perfect day to be on the lake. Making it even more special is being here with you! I can't believe we are here together in the place I've spent so many hours — in a place I love so much. This is fabulous!" She was really talking out loud to herself. Jim couldn't hear her over the noise of the engine. She got up from her seat and went over to him. She put her hand on his shoulder, leaned down and kissed him on the cheek.

"You missed my mouth," Jim declared. "You might want to try again." He grinned that special grin Susan had come to love. She patted him on the other shoulder, and followed his suggestion. He grinned again and suddenly turned the boat into a cove, stopping the engine. Susan had to hold on to the seat as the boat made the sudden turn and quick stop. The surprised look on her face changed as Jim got up out of his seat, took her in his arms and said, "There is something I want to know, Beautiful Prude. How many times have you been kissed on this lake?" He held on tightly with his face very close to hers.

She shifted a little, cleared her throat, and grinned widely. "Oh, Jim, why would you ask that right now? I don't know if I can answer that question quickly." She looked away from him with a thoughtful demeanor. He just smiled and waited patiently for her answer. She looked back at him and said, "It really could not have been more than two or three times, honestly."

"Oh. baby, come on — you know it was fifty times or more." Jim teased. "Anyone who looks like you surely had to spend all her life fighting off the guys!" Susan shook her head and withdrew from Jim's grasp. She walked over to the other side of the deck boat. Propping one knee on the seat, she leaned over the side of the boat to look at the water. It was a shallow cove. She was glad the boat did not have a deep hull. Jim had stopped to get drinks from the cooler.

"Jim, this cove is really shallow. Come look. I can see the bottom of the lake."

Jim moved quickly to look while he handed her a Diet Coke. "Yes, BP, it is shallow. Thank goodness, this is a deck boat."

"That's what I thought, too," Susan agreed. With a twinkle in her eye, she stood up. deposited her drink in the holder, and put her hands on Jim's shoulders. "Jim, would you believe me if I said that any kisses I might have had on this lake, in the light of *your* kisses, have sunk to the bottom of the lake, never to be thought of again?"

Her words pleased Jim immensely. Covering her hands with his he replied: "My dearest love, I do believe you, and I will not pry again about your past boyfriends. As long as I am the only man in your life now — besides your father — I am totally satisfied. As long as you promise from now on to kiss only your father and me, and any little boys we might have, I'm through with this line of questioning."

Susan laughed and ignored the part about the little boys. "You can be certain that you are the only man in my life beside my father. My kisses are reserved for you and daddy. I love you, Jim, and you alone." They embraced for a long time.

Eventually Jim returned to the captain's seat and started the boat again. As they skimmed across the water, he came up with an idea. "I think BP is a special name for you, babe, but let's change it to 'Beepie.' I think I like that better. What say you?" Jim asked, smiling.

"Well, that's somewhat surprising. But I think I like it, too. It will always mean something only you and I understand." Susan responded.

"Jim reached for her hand across the boat. She moved over to his seat and held onto the back of it with her other hand.

"Now, what shall I call *you*?" Susan pondered. "I don't think 'Hitch' is special enough."

"I'll leave it up to you," Jim answered. "You will think of one, I'm sure, Miss Beepie." He smiled as he called her his new pet name for her.

They continued their boat ride for another hour. Late that afternoon, since Susan didn't belong to the Country Club, they found a public community tennis court and played several sets. The rest of the evening passed by far too quickly. Soon it was time for Jim to go to his hotel room. Reluctantly they ended what had been a unique day for both. The next day they would travel to Susan's parents' home in Black Mountain, North Carolina, about an hour from Morganton, and fourteen miles east of Asheville.

CHAPTER TWENTY-THREE

CHAPTER TWENTY-THREE

THE drive from Morganton to Black Mountain was awesome. Though Morganton was surrounded by mountains, as they traveled I-40 toward Asheville, the elevation of the mountains increased. Not far from Black Mountain they found themselves in the midst of the beautiful Blue Ridge Mountains. The blue haze which hovered over the mountains confirmed that they had been correctly named. A stretch of the expressway wound around the mountains in such a way that it was necessary to slow down. Huge expanses of rock had been cut through by gigantic machines to allow travelers to cross over the mountains. One glorious mile followed the next as the highway twisted and turned through the magnificence of God's creation.

Everywhere one looked was a vista worth seeing. Susan reveled in the sight each time she saw it. It lifted her thoughts heavenward as she gazed in awe at God's marvelous handiwork. Jim had never traveled that direction on I-40. He could not find words to describe the beauty around him. He reached over and squeezed Susan's hand, noting that she, too, was at a loss for words.

Behind Black Mountain, Mt. Mitchell towered above the mountains surrounding it. Susan had climbed to the top once not too long ago. This was a memory she must share with Jim some time. The mountains stood mightily against the blue sky which today was interspersed with snowy white clouds. What a perfect backdrop for this memorable trip!

When they got to the Black Mountain exit, Susan directed Jim to her parents' home. On the way to their house they went through the quaint downtown area of Black Mountain. Cherry Street had become famous for antiques and good places to eat. Susan's favorite place was the *Veranda Café*, a tea room and boutique. The items for sale were things women loved — unusual jewelry, sweet-smelling soaps, beautiful linens, to name a few. Susan liked browsing in shops like this. Most items were too expensive for her pocketbook; but it was always fun to look.

Susan had a special connection with the old Hardware Store on Black Mountain's Main Street, which was in reality, Highway 70. She explained to Jim how that came about.

"One day when I was stopped at the stop light at that corner, I glanced over to the hardware store display window. I saw a little red fire engine — big enough for a child to sit in, and designed in great detail like a real one. Immediately I thought of my grandfather. How many times had he told us the story of losing his little red fire engine? It was his favorite toy when he was a little boy during World War II. It was sitting out in the front yard of his aunt's house on a day when the town was having a scrap metal collection. Mistakenly, the scrap collection guys thought it was left there to be picked up and donated. What a tragedy for a little boy to lose his most treasured toy!

Since this favorite toy had never been replaced, I came up with an idea. Why not get the grandchildren to go together at Christmas and give Grandpa a shiny, new red fire engine? That is just what we did! The hardware store ordered one; and it arrived just in time for Christmas. What a big surprise for Grandpa! He could hardly believe his eyes. His future great grandchildren would enjoy it for years to come!"

As Jim and Susan arrived at her parents' house, Jim saw that it was picture perfect. It rested at the foot of a mountain, across from tiny man-made Lake Tomahawk. Jim could hardly wait to hit the walking trail, circling the pond-like lake. The ducks had beaten him there; he was anxious to join them. But first things first. Meeting Susan's parents was his number one priority. After all, if he was about to become a part of the family, he needed to *meet* 'the family.' He thought to himself, *I hope they like me. They probably think Susan is taking an awful risk, getting serious when she's only known me a few days.*

Soon his fears dissipated. With smiles on their faces, Susan's mom and dad emerged from the front door as soon as they heard the car in the driveway. Immediately Jim knew where Susan got her good looks. She was a composite of these two handsome seniors. Susan's mom, Carolyn, was waving both hands. She was visibly excited and thrilled that they had come to visit. Her dad, though more reserved than her mom, connected with Jim as soon as they met. It was going to be a good weekend for both of them. At least it appeared that way.

After a delicious meal of Carolyn's superb home cooking, they all walked over to the lake. Jim and Susan put on walking shoes. While her parents sat on a bench and encouraged them in their journey, they walked around the lake three times. As the parents watched these two 'kids,' they shared their impressions of Susan's new 'love.' Later, Carolyn privately told Susan that they both thought Jim was a fine man — they liked him very much. They were looking forward to getting to know him better this weekend.

The plans for the afternoon included a tour of Biltmore Estate and dinner at the famous Grove Park Inn. Both were located in nearby Asheville. They planned to arrive at the Inn in time to eat on the terrace, watching the sun set over the Blue Ridge Mountains. This slow pace was a far cry from a normal Friday for Jim.

As they walked up another flight of steps at the Biltmore, it occurred to him that this slower pace suited him just fine. He didn't miss the rat race at all. Nor did he feel a longing for his typical Atlanta weekend. In his heart and soul at that moment, he was quite content. He came to attention again as he nearly stumbled over the top step. He caught hold of the railing just in time. Susan was at his side, trying to keep him from falling. "Are you okay?" she inquired.

"I don't know when I've been so 'okay,' Jim responded. "Why don't we build us a home like this?" he teased. "Do you think you would have enough room?"

"Maybe," Susan joined in the joviality. "But I think we would need an elevator. There are just too many steps."

"I agree. Be taking notes on what you like and don't like. I'll do the same." Jim said, as he put his arm around her and squeezed her for a moment. The tour was enjoyable for all. Jim had never been to the Biltmore before. What a spectacular place! The Vanderbilt's were far ahead of their time!

CHAPTER TWENTY-FOUR
CHAPTER TWENTY-FOUR

NOW, it was on to The Grove Park Inn, a favorite spot for everyone in the car. It had long been a family tradition of the Strasbourg's to have lunch on the terrace. Dinner there was thought to be too expensive. Tonight Jim would give them that special treat. It was a favorite place of his, too. He had brought more than one young lady here for the weekend.

When they arrived at the Grove Park Inn, everyone got out of Tom's car. He left his keys with the young man valet parking the cars. As Jim stood in front of the old hotel, a rush of sadness came over him. As he looked up at the huge expanse of red tile roof hovering over the massive stones covering the outer walls of the Inn, he began to think about his past. *What made me think sleeping with so many women was the 'way to live'? The fun was short-lived and the memories are only regrets. Here Susan is a virgin. She wants to save herself for her husband alone. I intend to be her husband. I think she wants to be my wife. How could I have done this to her — I'm going to give her a tarnished vessel of a husband. What a bum rap!*

Susan came around to where Jim was standing. "Isn't it awesome!" she remarked. "As many times as we've come, I always marvel at its beauty and wonder how they built this huge edifice without the equipment and tools we have today. In 1913, what tools did they have?" she asked. Jim turned his focus to her as they walked into the magnificent lobby with its two huge stone fireplaces flanking the expansive and comfortable greeting room. He began to explain to her how he thought they had built this remarkable hotel.

As they toured the hotel, thoughts of the past kept crossing Jim's mind. He didn't want to think about Dot and Marianne and Lisa — girls from his past. He only wanted to think about Susan — the girl of his present and future — the most wonderful girl he had ever known. *"God, please forgive me. I don't ever want to go back to that life."* Jim muttered under his breath. *"And please, God, help Susan to forgive me."* Jim wasn't much good at praying. At the moment, that was all he could think to do. If God didn't help him and Susan, they might not make it. She would probably agree on that one. *What is a girl like her doing here with a guy like me? If she knew I had brought those other girls here, would she walk out right now?* He thought she probably would.

Just then, Carolyn asked him a question he did not want to answer: "Jim, have you been here before?"

"Yes, I have, several times. It is really quite a place, isn't it?" Jim responded, trying not to reveal anything more. He could not imagine what they would think if they knew the truth. In spite of the turmoil raging within, at that moment Jim determined to put on a good 'front' and make the evening enjoyable for Susan and her folks.

As they walked through the vast lobby and entered the terrace, they all marveled at the gorgeous Mountain View before them. They heard the first strains of the melodious string quartet. What a fantastic setting for watching the sunset! They sat at a table for six because Robert, Susan's brother, was planning to join them for dinner. He was seventeen and had a summer job in Asheville. His mom and dad wanted Jim and Robert to meet. Jim knew he was very special to Susan. After all, she was eleven when he was born. She helped to raise him!

They had been seated only a few minutes when Robert

appeared in the doorway of the terrace. He located their table, and happily joined them. During the excellent meal, they engaged in lively conversations. Their interests centered on Atlanta, Morgantown, Black Mountain, and Asheville.

Jim was anxious to hear about Susan's growing up days. He encouraged them to share stories with him. He asked if they had any videos of Susan when she was younger.

"We might have two or three," Tom spoke up. "Mom, do you know where they are?"

"No, honey," she replied. "I will try to find them."

Robert interjected his thoughts at this point. "Jim might like to hear about your basketball career, Sister Sue." They all laughed at his pet name for Susan. "There are some neat stories about that," he added. "I've heard them so many times I can almost tell them myself. Mom was not too thrilled when Susan asked permission to join the basketball team. But God had another plan." He paused and turned to his mother. "Why don't you share about that, mom?"

By now, Jim was intrigued. He wanted to hear this story!

Tom joined in the conversation. "You could start with the Parents' Conference, Carolyn."

"Do you really want me to tell that story?" she asked Tom and Robert. They told her they did. Carolyn hesitated a minute; then she started her monologue.

"This is one experience I shall never forget!" she exclaimed. "When Susan was thirteen, she was involved in singing and dancing and drama. She was also very athletic; but her request for permission to be on the Middle School basketball team really caught us by surprise. Now, Jim, it might sound strange to you in this day and time, but I really didn't envision my pretty little daughter playing school sports. I thought she would continue doing artsy things. I really could not identify with her need to play basketball. I don't have an athletic bone in my body!" She paused while they laughed. Then she went on to say, "I really wanted God's best for her — I just didn't know what it was! Tom and I told her we would give her an answer the next day."

Carolyn continued: "The next day was a Saturday. We were scheduled to attend a Parenting Conference at our church in Morganton. An expert on parenting was the speaker. We had looked forward to it for months. Not surprisingly, his message that Saturday morning was based on Proverbs 22: 6: 'Train up a child in the way he should go, And when he is old, he will not depart from it.' After he quoted the verse, he gave us his interpretation of it: He believed that 'Training up a child in the way he should go not only meant in the way God planned for him to go, but also in the way the child was *bent* — in the way God had made him or her.' He gave us parents some advice. He said: 'If your daughter is athletic, you should seriously consider letting her participate in sports. If your son likes English and literature, let him concentrate on those subjects.' I was stunned! I never expected to hear those words that Saturday morning!"

"I knew at that moment God was speaking to me. I needed to be willing for our daughter to play basketball. After all, that was the way God made her! When we got home from the conference, we gave Susan our permission to be on the basketball team. "You were thrilled, weren't you, Susan?!" Susan nodded. "For the next six years she played on school teams. We loved watching her play, attending as many games as possible. Has Susan told you the position she played on every team, Jim?" Carolyn asked.

"Point guard, I believe," Jim replied as he patted Susan on the shoulder. "I hope you have some of her games on video!"

"Mom," Robert quickly interrupted, "you didn't tell us what else happened at the conference! You didn't tell us about your unusual prayer!"

Carolyn had not planned to share that part of the story. When Robert brought it up, she had to make a decision. She turned to Susan and asked, "Is it okay for me to tell this part of the story, or would you rather tell Jim yourself?" Her mom obviously did not want to embarrass Susan.

"It's fine for you to tell it, Mom," Susan answered. "You are the one with the firsthand version!" Susan laughed.

Tom spoke again. "If you share your prayer, you certainly must share the first answer to your prayer which occurred at Susan's last ballgame, mother! I think Jim would enjoy hearing about both!"

Susan glanced at Jim. She remembered this story so well because her mother had repeated it many times in her presence. She wondered how Jim would react to what he was about to hear. There was a quizzical look on Jim's face. He could not imagine why Tom and Robert were urging Susan's mom to share something that sounded to him like a personal and private experience. He smiled at Susan and waited.

With the urging of her family, Carolyn, in a rather shy voice began 'the rest of the story.' She told them: "In the prayer time at the end of the conference, I prayed and surrendered to God's will and His plan for Susan. I decided to add my own request to God, too. Let's see. I'm pretty sure these were my exact words. 'Lord, I will let Susan play basketball, but would You help her always to be a reflection of Your glory and a gracious Southern lady?'"

Carolyn looked at Tom for support. "Do you want me to continue?" she asked everyone. They all nodded and listened intently as she shared how God had first answered that prayer. She told them, "The first answer to this prayer came during Susan's last basketball game her senior year in high school. We were sitting in the stands at halftime. A team mother walked over to where we were sitting and sat on the empty bench behind us. She leaned over and said to me, 'Carolyn, I want to tell you something I've been thinking about for several weeks. Everyone knows you have a beautiful daughter, but let me tell you something else I've observed this year. Susan has been a great role model for the other girls on the team. She really lives by her convictions! You must be so proud of her, Carolyn. She is such a lady!'"

"Oh, mom, that's enough! Now I *am* embarrassed," Susan exclaimed.

"Well, you shouldn't be, Sus. That woman was telling your mom the truth," Jim stated emphatically. Susan was surprised, but thankful for his reaction. He reached over, put his arm around her, and kissed her on the cheek. "What she told your mom doesn't surprise me at all," Jim declared. "Thank you for sharing that, Carolyn! It is a great story!"

By this time the sunset was at its peak. They all turned and looked toward the mountains. As the sun began to slip behind the mountains, Susan leaned over and took Jim's hand in hers. "It's so beautiful tonight. I used to dream about coming here someday with the most special person in my life. It's better than I even dreamed it would be. Thank you, Jim, for bringing us here tonight."

Jim smiled, but inside his guilt was intensifying. He gulped and tried to suppress the bad feelings that were seeking to engulf him. He prayed Susan would not be able to tell of his discomfort. Actually, he was feeling both discomfort and disdain — disdain for those wasted years and discomfort in the presence of her purity and goodness. Could they really 'make it' as a couple, he wondered. When he told her about his past — and he knew he had to — would she still want to marry him? Tonight, he could not shake the fear and sadness, no matter how he tried. Susan was so enthralled with everything she didn't seem to notice his doleful demeanor.

After dinner, Jim and Susan walked down the steps of the Inn to look around and view the beauty of the place, now illuminated for the evening. Jim stopped on one of the decks and turned to face Susan. He placed both hands on her shoulders and looked longingly into her brown eyes. "Oh, Beepie," he finally said. "Do you have any idea how much I love you?"

"I think I do, Jim, because I know how much I already love you." Jim pulled her to him. They stayed in that embrace for a long time. When he released her, he kissed the top of her head and took her hand once more. "There is no way I can tell you how I feel, tonight, Sus. Just know that I would rather be here with *you* than anyone else in the whole world!" He strongly declared. She could not possibly know how guilty he felt for not telling her about the others. This was not the time or place. Suffice it to say that he had told her what he wanted her to hear — he wanted so badly for her to hear the heart of the 'reformed' guy she was in love with. Because of her, Jim's lifestyle had changed in a matter of hours. He had found the love of his life, and that had changed everything. He would tell her about his past at the appropriate time. He would spend the rest of his life trying to become the man she deserved. It would not be easy; but he would certainly try.

CHAPTER TWENTY-FIVE
CHAPTER TWENTY-FIVE

ON Saturday morning, Jim and Susan's dad were scheduled to play golf at the Black Mountain Golf Course. Susan and her mom planned a shopping trip in Black Mountain. They would all go to Billy Graham's Cove that afternoon. This well-known Billy Graham retreat center was a favorite of the Strasbourg's. Their family took great delight in attending seminars at The Cove. They loved to visit the Chapel built especially for the Grahams.

After their visit to the Cove, the Strasbourg's suggested that Jim and Susan spend the rest of Saturday by themselves. That idea sounded great to them. They decided to go over to Lake Lure. Jim had never been there, and Susan wanted him to see it. The curvy mountain road made traveling slower than Jim was accustomed to. They finally arrived at Lake Lure Inn at sunset. When Jim saw the Inn, he made a decision: The first night of their honeymoon must be spent at this quaint hotel on the banks of Lake Lure. The area surrounding it was an awesome Switzerland-like place! It was delightful! No wonder Susan was so fond of this unique spot. He decided to keep it a secret and surprise his bride on their wedding night. He knew she would love it.

SUNDAY morning dawned bright and beautiful. Susan and Jim joined her parents at a small church in Black Mountain. Everywhere the rhododendrons were blooming. Susan loved seeing them in full bloom. Her favorite color was purple. Her mother's back yard had always been filled with those big purple blooms.

That afternoon, even though they were not ready to leave, the time had come for parting. Jim asked to speak with Tom privately before they left. When they found a private spot beside the house, Jim spoke, trying not to be too forward, "I guess, Tom, you might have figured out by now that I'm in love with your daughter and want to marry her."

"Well, Jim, I thought that might be the case," Tom responded, smiling.

"Mr. Strasbourg, I didn't know it was possible to fall for someone so quickly. But the night I met Susan, I felt certain I had met the love of my life. She is the most amazing woman I have ever known. I never dreamed she would be able to love me like I do her — at least not so quickly. But I believe she does, and I want to marry her." Jim cleared his throat and continued haltingly. "I would like to ask your permission and blessing." He couldn't believe he had actually gotten out those words. But it was something he felt he had to do before they left Black Mountain.

Tom responded quickly. "Yes, Jim, if this is your desire *and* Susan's, I certainly will give my permission and blessing. The only thing I would say is to be sure you are on the same page in every possible area, especially in your religious beliefs. If you don't agree on those beliefs, you should not consider marriage." Then he added with a slight smile, "Carolyn and I will certainly be praying daily for you both. Thank you for asking my permission and blessing." He shook Jim's hand wholeheartedly.

"Thank you, sir, very much. We will give serious thought to your words. And I promise you that I will try to take as good care of your daughter as you have all these years. Susan is very precious to me. She will always be my greatest priority." Jim stated sincerely.

With a glint in his eye and a knowing smile on his face, Jim walked back to where Susan and Carolyn were standing. He placed his arm on Susan's and gave her a huge smile. Then he turned to Carolyn and Tom and hugged them both, thanking them profusely for their wonderful hospitality. "It has been a great weekend, folks. Thanks for all you've done for us." Jim said.

"We've loved having you here," Carolyn responded. "We look forward to your next visit."

"We'll be back as soon as possible, won't we Sus?" Jim asked. "I'll be coming back to North Carolina every chance I get!" Jim exclaimed. He pulled Susan to him and they all smiled.

"We will be praying for your safe trips back to Morganton and Atlanta," Tom added. With smiles on their faces, Susan and Jim opened the car doors and got in. Jim started the car, and pulled out of the driveway. All were waving good-bye. They had not gone too far before Jim reached over to take Susan's hand and declared in a loud voice, "He said 'yes,' my love! Your daddy said 'yes'! Great balls of fire, Susan, there is going to be a wedding in the near future!" and he leaned over and kissed the cheek of one very flustered and thrilled North Carolina belle.

"You asked my daddy if you could marry me?" Susan asked incredulously.

"Yes ma'am, I did, and he said 'yes'! Are you surprised?" Jim asked, smiling.

"About your asking him or about his reply?" Susan asked.

"About either one or both," Jim answered.

"I guess I'm surprised about both ... but very, very happy, my darling!" Susan answered and leaned over, touching his arm with her hand and his cheek with her lips. "I love you, Jim Hitchenson, and I always will."

"I love you, Susan Strasbourg, and I always will — forever and ever and ever. My forever love. That's what you are — my forever love." Jim responded enthusiastically. This was not the time to think about her dad's admonition to him. This was a time for celebration!

THE weekend was over. It was time to fly back to Atlanta. Jim knew his life would never be the same! At last he was going to get married! His mom would be thrilled that Susan was his choice. Susan would be coming the next weekend for Violet's and Dan's wedding. He could not help but wish it were theirs instead of Violet's.

Susan fretted all week over what to wear for the rehearsal dinner and the wedding. She finally decided to wear a green outfit on Friday night and a blue one to the wedding. Jim loved for her to wear anything blue!

When Jim picked her up at Violet's house, it was obvious he was very happy with the way she looked. To him, she always looked beautiful! They eagerly drove to this special event. The wedding was not a disappointment! It seemed just perfect to Susan. Violet and Dan were so in love. Their circuitous path to the wedding altar had not cast any kind of shadow on this special night. If anything, the time they had spent apart, had served only to draw them closer. Now, they could truly be one — in every way.

At the wedding reception, it seemed everyone wanted to meet Susan — Jim's 'new love.' It was a fabulous night for the bride and groom, and a fantastic night for the bride-to-be and her future husband. That is, until a certain 'friend' of Jim's decided to bring the festivities to a halt — at least for Jim and Susan. Myrtle Mayhall, longtime friend of the family, sauntered over to where Susan was standing. Smiling a 'knowing' smile, she introduced herself to Susan. Jim was talking to another old friend and did not see her or hear what she said to Susan.

"Susan, you don't know me, but I'm a lifelong friend of the Hitchenson's. I've been in Paris for several years. I just happened to be back in the States for this wedding. I don't know you very well; but I know Jim real well. Everyone here tonight tells me you and Jim are about to get married."

"It looks that way, Myrtle," Susan answered, smiling.

"Well, as one friend to another, I think I need to tell you something I don't think you know. Jim may have told you he plans to marry you. But he also asked my cousin in New York City to marry him. Did you know that?"

Susan's face was by this time white as a sheet. She felt sick inside, and thought she would faint. "No, I didn't," she replied in disbelief. "How would you happen to have that information?" Susan questioned her, getting more and more upset every second.

"Because my cousin told me he asked her," Myrtle answered. "I just thought you ought to know before you went and did something you would live to regret."

As Jim turned around, what he saw was a shocker: Susan was almost running to the nearest exit. He immediately went after her, wondering what on earth was happening. As he neared the door he heard Myrtle's voice, "Jim, since you didn't own up to the fact that you had another woman, I told her."

Jim stopped and whirled around, grabbing Myrtle by the shoulders, "You what?" Jim asked in disbelief.

"I told her you had proposed to my cousin and she had said 'yes.'" Myrtle answered.

Jim was incredulous. He emphatically declared, "We were both drunk, Myrtle, and you know it! Neither one of us has ever talked about it again! That was six or seven years ago. You know she didn't think I was serious. I haven't seen or heard from her in years!" Jim was visibly upset. "My word, Myrtle, what is wrong with you?" He jerked away and ran for the door, looking for Susan.

When he found her, she was crying uncontrollably. It seemed she could not stop herself. He put his arms around her, but she pulled away. "Just leave me alone, Jim. It seems your *past* always catches up with me — wherever I go." Her tears poured forth like a tiny waterfall.

Jim stood speechless for a moment. His heart was about to break in two. He gently reached out to Susan again and pulled her down on the park bench beside him. "Please hear me out, Susan." He tried to take her hands in his, but she kept her back toward him. "I'm not sure why girls like Myrtle seem to reappear in my life to try and spoil everything. Myrtle lived down the street when I was growing up. She was always jealous of Vi. Her cousin Lisa came and visited her often. The two of them decided many years ago that I was the one for Lisa. As we got older, we partied a lot. One night Lisa and I were both drunk. I told her that after all these years, maybe we just needed to get married. She agreed. What I didn't know was that she was in love with me. She told Myrtle that I had proposed. That was six or seven years ago. I haven't seen her or talked to her since then. I never thought she took it seriously — we were both drunk, for goodness sake. Susan, that is the truth, I promise you," Jim concluded emphatically.

Susan did not respond. After a minute, Jim got up and turned in the direction of the ballroom. He needed to settle this matter ASAP. "I am going to find Myrtle and bring her out here. Together, we are going to call Lisa and put an end to this nonsense once for all," he declared as he dashed toward the reception hall.

It was very late when they were able to get Lisa, Myrtle's cousin, on the phone. Jim turned on the speaker so all could hear her. When Jim told Lisa what had happened, she just laughed and replied: "You are too late, Jim. Phil and I eloped last week. We had been dating for five years and decided it was time we married." She continued, "I knew you weren't serious when you suggested we should get married. I never took it seriously. We were both drunk. I'm sorry, Jim. Please apologize to your fiancée. I'm just glad you found somebody." Lisa had settled the issue once and for all.

Myrtle had listened in on the conversation, too. Now she stood speechless. Jim grabbed Susan and glared at Myrtle as he said, "Let's get out of here!"

What else was going to happen before she and Jim could get married, Susan wondered, as she flew back to Morganton on Sunday night. Were these things God's warnings to her that she should not marry Jim? How could she and Jim love each other so much if their relationship was not 'meant to be'?

She bowed her head and prayed: "Lord, if I'm headed down the wrong road, please stop me. I don't want to continue in this relationship if Jim and I are not to be husband and wife. Lord, I love him more than life itself. Oh, how I love Jim Hitchenson! Show me the way, O dear Lord. Please show me the way!"

She kept her eyes closed; before she knew it, the stewardess was telling her to put her seat up. As she was righting her seat, Jim's nickname came to her: She would call him 'Hitchie.' That was it —'Hitchie.' She could hardly wait to tell him! Would he like it? She hoped so!

CHAPTER TWENTY-SIX

CHAPTER TWENTY-SIX

THE week began normally for Susan. She wasn't expecting any surprises this week. Jim had a business trip to Washington; he was going to be exceptionally busy. She had several new accounts to take care of; she would be busy, too. On Tuesday her cell phone rang about eleven o'clock. It was Jim calling. "Hello there," she answered. "Are you *en route* to Washington?"

"Actually," Jim replied, "I am just landing at the airport — the airport in Morganton."

Susan gasped: "Why are you landing here? Is there a problem with your plane?" Morganton had a tiny airport. Only small planes regularly used their landing strip.

"No, ma'am," Jim replied with a voice that sounded quizzical. "There is not a problem with anything except that I need to see you very badly." This time he sounded like himself. He added, "Do you think you could bring me some lunch?"

Stunned for a moment, Susan recovered and replied, "Of course, I can do that. What do you want me bring?"

"How about a roast beef sandwich from that deli we went to?" Jim asked in answer to her question.

"Oh, yes, that would be great," Susan said. "I'll be there in just a few minutes. Where do I come?" she asked, still in disbelief that this was really happening. Jim asked for directions and gave her the correct information. He grinned as he put his cell phone in his pocket; Susan had no idea why he had really stopped here at the Morganton airport this morning. She would soon find out!

Susan arrived in about twenty minutes with their lunch, excited and amazed that she was about to see Jim! When he saw her car drive up, he hurried down the stairs of his plane and met her half way. He was wearing a very happy face. When he reached her, he grabbed her in a big hug, mashing the sacks of food she was carrying. Ignoring what he had done, he kissed her fervently. Soon he was taking her hand, escorting her to the steps of his private jet. Taking the bags of food in one hand, he used the other to help her climb the steep stairs.

They laughed and talked as they ate. Both were obviously thrilled to be in each other's company once more. Susan certainly didn't know why he had made this detour on his trip; but it was an awesome surprise!

After they had eaten, Jim told her he needed to get something. He walked a few feet to a small closet. When he returned he had a gift bag in his hand. The look on his face revealed that he was 'up to something big.' Sitting down across from her, he leaned forward and said, "I brought you a little something I want you to have." Then he grinned as he put his hand down into the bag and retrieved a small black box.

Susan was getting more excited by the minute. Jim placed the box between his knees. He reached for her hands, pulled her toward him, and gently kissed her lips. "Oh, my Beautiful Prude, I love you so. I decided I couldn't wait any longer to give you this." Letting go of her hands, he picked up the box and opened it. There was a red velvet box inside. Looking into her eyes with all the love he felt in his heart, he fell to his knees, and asked, "Susan Strasbourg, will you do me the honor of marrying me?" He opened the box to reveal an absolutely gorgeous diamond engagement ring.

Susan's eyes nearly popped out of her head. "Oh, Jim, oh Jim, oh Jim," was all she could say.

When she didn't say 'yes,' he asked again, "Darling, will you marry me?"

Susan pulled him toward her and replied, "Oh, yes, my love, of course I will marry you! I love you with all my heart; but for a moment there, I was too stunned to speak sensibly." Jim breathed a sigh of relief as he brought her lips to his.

Jim pulled back to open the ring box once more. He put the ring on her finger, saying, "Susan, I love you more than I ever thought it was possible to love anyone. I know it may be a scary thing to think about giving yourself completely to me. But there is nothing I want more than to give myself completely to you and have you do the same to me," and their lips found each other again. For a time they reveled in the glory of this momentous occasion.

Suddenly Jim asked, "Don't you want to go back to my bedroom for a little while? Now, that we're engaged."

Susan smiled and said, "You know better than that, Jim Hitchenson. I love you more than life itself. I can hardly wait to be your wife; but we have an agreement, I believe, and I intend to keep my part of the bargain."

Susan got up to go. Jim stood and embraced her once more. "Thank you for bringing me lunch and agreeing to marry me," Jim finally said with a great big smile.

"Thank you for asking me — to bring you lunch — and to marry you!" She held up her hand to show him the gorgeous ring which now adorned it. "My ring is gorgeous — I've never seen one more exquisite!"

"I hoped you would like it," Jim told her as he escorted her down the steps of his plane and walked her to her car. Reluctantly, they bade each other good-bye. Jim had a meeting in Washington at three o'clock. Unfortunately, it was time for him to go!

When Susan got back to the office, the employees couldn't believe their eyes. As they talked about it later they agreed with one of the employees who said, "I am not sure which was shining more brightly — the huge diamond on her finger or the sparkle in Susan's eyes." All at once, with a sad look on his face, one of the guys verbalized his feelings: "We are about to lose our boss!" The big question now, was when?

CHAPTER TWENTY-SEVEN

CHAPTER TWENTY-SEVEN

JIM was to be gone to Europe for a week. That would give Susan additional time to prepare for their wedding. When he returned, she was to join him in Atlanta for a party or two. Everything was moving along nicely until Tuesday about ten AM when Susan's office phone rang. It was Fred Moseley, her pastor. "What a nice surprise to hear from you, Fred. What can I do for you, today?" Susan asked.

Fred replied: "I wondered if you might be free for lunch. I know it is last minute, but I really need to see you as soon as possible." He sounded worried about something.

"Yes," she responded. "I am free. Where would you like to meet?" They settled on a restaurant near Susan's office. As she hung up the phone her curiosity was piqued. She wondered why he wanted to see her — and why so urgently. About half an hour before noon, she gathered her things and left the office. As she got into her car, she realized her stomach was churning. She suddenly had a sense that Fred was upset about something that involved her. She drove quickly to the restaurant. Fred was already seated and waiting for her when she got there.

"Hi, Fred. So good to see you. How have you been?" Susan asked, trying to appear calm.

"Oh, things at the church are running smoothly right now. I am always grateful for that." Just then the waiter came to take their drink order. Fred spied Susan's engagement ring and commented on its beauty. Then his countenance changed, and he gave her a somber look. "Susan, your marriage to Jim is why I asked you to meet me. I might as well tell you up front what's on my mind."

Susan was startled. "What in the world, Fred? Why do you want to talk about my marriage?" By this time Susan was experiencing some distress.

"I don't know for certain, Susan, but the last few days I've been thinking about you and Jim so much. Before I marry a couple. I really do like to counsel with them. Since you've not mentioned it, I felt that I should. Is there a time when Jim could come before the wedding? I would like to ask him some questions and do a little premarital counseling." Fred replied.

Susan sighed and relaxed. "Oh, is that all, Fred? Why certainly I'm sure we can work that in before the wedding."

The waiter's arrival was a welcome break. After he left, Fred picked up the conversation again. "I'm happy to hear that, Susan. I'm sure you and Jim have discussed his relationship with the Lord. But before I marry a couple, I need to know for certain that both are Christians. You know how strongly I feel about a couple being 'unequally yoked.'"

"Of course, I know that, Fred. I feel exactly the same way. God speaks very strongly against being 'unequally yoked' with an unbeliever. You know I would never want that. Jim is a fine Christian man; I don't think we will have a problem with the fact that we belong to different churches. We'll be able to work that out, I'm certain," Susan sought to assure him.

"I would suggest strongly that you try to determine where you will attend church before you are married. That way, you don't have to wrestle with that problem after marriage. You will have enough adjustments to deal with. You don't need that one." Fred went on to say.

"Thank you for suggesting that, Fred. We'll do just that. We may decide not to go to either of our denominations, but find another that fits us better. There are so many churches in Atlanta; I don't think that will be much of a challenge for us." Just then Fred and Susan's lunch arrived. She changed the subject. For the rest of the meal they had casual conversation. When they had eaten, Susan told Fred she had to get back to the office. She thanked him for lunch and headed out the door.

When she got into her car, closed the door, and put the key in the ignition, Fred's words came back to her like a hammer's blow to her heart: "*Before I marry a couple I need to know for certain that both are Christians.*" A panicky feeling came over her as Fred's words flowed through her mind: "K*now for certain, know for certain, know for certain ...* "

For the first time Susan realized that she did *not* know for certain Jim was truly saved. She had never asked him. He had never volunteered any such information. She had just assumed he was a born-again believer. She started the engine and headed for the office. She was so upset by the time she got to the office, she hardly spoke to the employees. Heading straight to her desk, she shut the door behind her. She slumped into her chair. "W*hat is wrong with me? Of course, Jim is a Christian. I would never have fallen in love with an unbeliever! We just haven't talked about it. And we need to. We'll talk tonight.*"

Nagging thoughts would not leave, no matter how Susan tried to put them out of her mind. What if he's not a Christian? What if he was just confirmed in the Episcopal Church? What if he doesn't believe what I believe about the Bible being God's Holy Word? The questions began to come fast and furious. Questions to which she realized she had no answer. When Jim finally called late that night, Susan could hardly contain herself. She had so many questions to ask Jim; but she could not ask them over the phone. He was too far away. This wasn't the time. She would wait until he got home.

As the week progressed, Susan became increasingly anxious

about Jim's relationship with the Lord and about their future. She called Fred on Friday morning and asked to see him that day or the next. He sensed her anxiety and asked her to come to his office at the church. As Susan and Fred started to talk, she began to cry. "Oh, Fred, what have I done?" she cried. "I fell in love with Jim so quickly and never once stopped to ask him about his relationship with the Lord. How could I have been so foolish? All I ever wanted was to have a husband who would be a strong Christian and a loving father for my children." Then she blurted out, "Fred, I don't know whether Jim is a believer or not! His lifestyle certainly doesn't match up to that of a true believer. Maybe I just convinced myself he was a Christian who had rebelled. What am I going to do, Fred, what am I going to do?" She asked as she bowed her head and sobbed softly.

Fred got up and came over to her, placing his hand on her shoulder. He began to pray for her out loud. "Father, here your precious daughter sits — not knowing what to do or say. This has not taken You by surprise. You knew she would come to this point. I believe You have stopped her in her tracks so that she would know and do Your will. Speak to her heart at this moment. Give her Your peace and comfort and strength. In Jesus' Name, Amen."

CHAPTER TWENTY-EIGHT
CHAPTER TWENTY-EIGHT

SUSAN spent most of the weekend in great anguish with tears flowing endlessly. She felt exceedingly guilty that she had allowed her relationship with Jim to reach this point. She loved him with all her heart and wanted to marry him. She would not do so without knowing where he stood with the Lord. In her heart she knew she must confront him. But How? When? Where?

Each time he called it got harder for her not to talk to him about this. She didn't know how much longer she could hide her anxiety and despair. Jim was coming back Sunday night. She was to come to Atlanta on Tuesday. Finally, on Sunday afternoon, she made a decision. She would tell him she could not come. She needed more time to think.

When she told him on the phone Sunday night of her decision, he was speechless. "Susan, what in the world is going on? You can't do this to me — to us. We've been apart a whole week, and it has been awful! I need to see you!" Jim rambled on about his dismay at her decision.

"I don't know how to tell you what I am feeling, Jim. I just don't think we need to see each other this week. I need more time." Susan knew her words were not convincing Jim this was the best thing for them to do, but she could think of no other way to handle her fears and anxieties.

Jim wanted to come to Morganton, but Susan would not agree. For the first time, their phone conversation was about to end with Jim being very angry. No matter how she had pleaded for him to understand, he simply could not seem to. He was frustrated and angry and fearful. "Baby, you can't keep me away longer! I don't understand!" he cried out as he slammed the phone down.

When Susan tried to get him on the phone again, he would not answer. She cried out to the Lord in her grief and despair. She just couldn't lose Jim now! "O *God, please help me. I don't know what to do!*" The only person she felt free to call was her mother. Carolyn would be a sounding board as well as a good counselor. Her mom answered on the first ring.

Meanwhile in Atlanta, Jim was pacing up and down the floor of his condo. He was totally baffled and greatly distressed. Not knowing which way to turn or what to do, Jim called Bill. Since it seemed Bill could not help him, he called Violet. She urged him to come over. For the next two hours they attempted to give him wise counsel. Before Jim left, Dan prayed earnestly for him and Susan.

After talking and praying with them, Jim decided not to press the issue any more. He was angry, frustrated and in disbelief. He had no idea what was happening; but they had advised him to 'cool it' for a little while longer. He kept telling himself this was only a temporary stoppage — Susan was just scared to 'make the plunge.' Violet had told him, "Jim, you don't want to marry someone who is not sure she loves you. You don't want to make a mistake and end up divorced. You hate divorce. Isn't it better to wait a few more days than to go forward against Susan's better judgment?"

He had finally agreed; but he was not happy about it at all. He could not let himself believe Susan did not love him. He knew deep down in his heart she did. What kind of stunt was she pulling? Why would she do this to the man she loved? It made no sense at all. For the first time since he had met Susan, he felt pulled to his old ways. More than anything else, he wanted a drink. Yes, that's what he needed — he needed to drown his sorrows in drink!

That thought played regularly in his head until Wednesday, when he finally gave way to his feelings. Against his better judgment, he went to his favorite bar and ordered a drink. He got so drunk, the bartender called for a taxi to take him to his yacht. When they arrived at the yacht, the taxi driver helped him get on board, leaving him slumped in a chair.

Meanwhile, Susan had driven to Atlanta. She wanted desperately to see Jim. If only she could spot him somewhere. She needed to talk to him in person! On Wednesday morning, she had gone to his boat and taped to the entrance post a long letter with the envelope addressed to him. Then she had gone to a friend's house to stay and pray.

When the taxi driver had taken Jim to his boat, he saw the envelope. As he and Jim were getting on the boat, he grabbed the envelope and stuck it in Jim's pocket. Later when Jim shifted in his chair, he felt it sticking out of his pocket.

JIM suddenly roused to see what was sticking out of his pocket. The first thing he noticed was that it smelled like Susan's favorite perfume. He tore open the envelope and tried to read the letter that was in it. When he realized he was sitting in the dark, he got up, stumbled into the living room and turned on a light. He grabbed the arm of the sofa and sprawled out on it. The writing was blurry, but he could not miss her words. "My darling Jim," he read. "When you get this, you will know that I have been to the boat because I could not bear to be away from you any longer. I thought if I just came here, I could catch a glimpse of you, or feel your breath on my face, even in my imagination. I have never been so miserable in my whole life. You are my life and I miss you more every moment. I don't want to be anywhere but with you. You are my only love and the one I love more than I ever thought it would be possible."

Jim had sat up by this time. Big tears began to roll down his face. *Where are you, Susan? I have to see you now!!* The shame of his drunkenness overwhelmed him. He tried to find his phone. He didn't need to read further. She had already written what he needed to hear. He had to talk to her right now!

Finally, locating his phone, he dialed her number. It rang several times. When he heard her voice, he cried out, "Oh, baby, where are you? I have to see you now!" His slurred speech betrayed his inebriated condition. He knew she could tell he was drunk.

"Oh, Jim, oh Jim," she answered with a sob.

"Susan, I'm so sorry. I'm so sorry. How can you ever forgive me? I was just so miserable, I couldn't handle it. Don't you know I can't make it without you, baby?"

"I'm the one who's sorry. I handled things so badly. I'm so glad you called. Did you get my letter?" she inquired.

"Yes, baby. Oh, yes, Sus, I did," Jim answered. There was a long pause. Then Susan spoke once more.

"Jim, as much as I want to see you, I don't think we should see each other until morning, do you?"

"No, baby, you're right." Jim replied sorrowfully. "But I want to see you so badly … where are you?"

"Jim, I'm here in Atlanta. Why don't I come to the boat in the morning?" Susan asked.

"Oh yes, baby. As early as you can get here," Jim replied. "Susan, I need you desperately. I don't want to live without you."

"Jim, let's not talk anymore. You need to sleep and I do, too. I'll see you in the morning, my love. Good night, Jim." Susan finished and hung up the phone. She couldn't stop crying. She spoke to her friend standing nearby: "It's my fault that he drank again. I have made such a mess of things!" When she had finally calmed down, she called Fred. He told her he would drive to Atlanta and meet her the next morning.

CHAPTER TWENTY-NINE
CHAPTER TWENTY-NINE

SUSAN and Fred met at a restaurant near the Marina. Before they got into their cars, they prayed and asked for wisdom and guidance in the hours ahead. Susan was a 'basket case' by now; only God could 'un-mess this mess.' How she prayed that He would. She wanted to marry Jim Hitchenson more than anything else in the world — but she could not and would not marry an unbeliever!

The gangplank was down when they arrived at the boat. They walked across it and went to the deck. Looking through the windows, Susan saw that the living room was dark. Evidently Jim was still asleep. They decided not to knock, but to wait on the deck until they saw movement inside the boat.

Before long, Jim got up and made himself some coffee. His head was pounding. He took a shower and started getting dressed. As he buttoned his shirt, he came into the kitchen for his coffee. It was then that he saw Susan and Fred. Immediately, he threw open the door to the deck and called out to Susan. She was in his arms almost before he took his next breath. Jim kissed her and hugged her and laughed out loud at the joy he felt to have her back in his arms. Susan just kept saying, "Oh, Jim, Oh, Jim, Oh, Jim."

Finally, Jim released her from his embrace and took her hand. "Let's get some coffee and talk," Jim said. Then it 'hit' him that someone was with Susan. Panic attacked him as he asked who was with her.

"Jim, that's Fred Moseley, my Pastor. He drove this morning from Morganton to be here for both of us."

"Don't we need to ask him to join us?" Jim recovered and asked.

"No, not yet," Susan responded. "Let's talk first." Jim went to the kitchen and nervously poured her a cup of coffee, spilling a few drops on the kitchen counter. He was still feeling the effects of the night before. Susan took the cup and walked into the living room, plopping down on one end of the sofa. After Jim had refilled his cup, he joined her. It was time for Susan to reveal to Jim the truth of their situation, no matter how difficult it might be.

Her fervent desire was to convey her feelings and beliefs in a way Jim would understand. She first told him of her convictions and of how conflicted she had been. She shared with him how upset she had become thinking they might be 'unequally yoked.' The number one thing she did not want to do was to lock Jim into a marriage he would regret all his life — having to live a lifestyle that was not his choice — feeling pressured into doing things her way.

Her words were very upsetting to Jim. He could not understand fully what she was saying. He was quite puzzled about part of it. For a few minutes he said nothing. Then he took both of her hands in his and said: "Susan, I love you more than life itself. You are the only girl I have ever wanted to marry. I want to marry you and live with you and love you and be the father of your children. I want nothing else. I have believed that is what you want, too. Am I wrong?" Jim asked.

"You know you are not wrong. There is nothing I want more than to marry you, Jim," Susan answered as she put her head on his shoulder for a moment.

Jim straightened up, put his fingers under her chin and

gently lifted her head so he could look into her eyes. Then he confessed, "I've never heard anyone talk about this 'unequally yoked' business before. I don't even understand what you're saying. But I am willing to do whatever you say I must do so you'll marry me. I *am* going to marry you. You are mine and I do not intend to ever let you go. So tell me what you want me to do." Jim exclaimed.

Susan was dumbstruck. She didn't know what to say next. How was she going to handle this delicate situation? She breathed a silent prayer and slowly, carefully responded: "Jim, I want to know if there has been a time in your life when you had a personal encounter with Jesus Christ and asked Him to be your Savior and Lord?"

Jim was stunned. He pulled back, made a face and replied, "What do you mean 'a personal encounter with Christ?' When I was twelve years old, I was confirmed. Is that what you mean?" he asked quizzically.

"You might have been 'born again' at that time. Of course, you could have, Jim. That is what I am asking you. Did you receive Jesus into your life when you were confirmed?" Susan anxiously inquired.

Jim was beginning to show his exasperation. "Now, I don't know how you expect me to know that, Sus! That was so many years ago. Aren't those just *words* you are using? Confirmed — born again. It's all the same, isn't it?" Jim begged. He made a face, got up from the sofa and retreated to his favorite chair.

Susan stopped. Her heart sank. She realized she was getting nowhere. Trying to hide her deep sorrow, she stood up and began to pace around the room, glancing at Fred and the ocean beyond. "*God, please help me right now. I need Your wisdom. I don't want Jim to be upset with me.*" Immediately the story of Violet and Dan came to her mind. If Jim would understand anything, he would understand that.

"Jim," Susan walked over to Jim's chair, breaking the

uncomfortable silence. "Think about Vi and Dan's situation for a minute. Why did Dan break their engagement?"

Jim thought a minute and then replied, "Well, because they didn't have the same goals and beliefs, I guess. Violet didn't think they were on the same wave link or something like that."

"That's it, my darling." Susan replied as she knelt at his feet, and reached for his hands. "I just want to be so sure we have the same goals and beliefs and are on the same wave link. I want us to be united physically, emotionally and spiritually. I know the first two won't be a problem; I just don't want the third to cause us difficulty later on."

Jim kissed her soundly then lifted her up and kissed her again. He held her in his arms for a very long time. When he spoke again, he said, "Now I understand. You want me to do what Dan did — get saved. Then you'll marry me."

Susan stepped back in surprise and said, "Yes, Jim. I want you to be saved; but I don't want you to do something just so I'll marry you." Susan walked away with tears streaming down her face. She realized that Jim now knew what she wanted of him; but would he 'go through the motions' for her sake? What should she do? What should she say?

She walked out on the deck where Fred was seated. Her countenance revealed her state of mind. "It's hopeless, Fred. I don't think we can work it out." Susan said, with feelings of despair and defeat. "I don't want him to pray a prayer he doesn't really mean so I'll marry him. Will you talk with him?" She hurriedly began to climb the steps to the upper deck. Her tears flowed freely, blurring her vision. She grasped hold of the rail to keep her balance. She had lost her hope of reconciliation with Jim. *"Oh, Lord, is it really over?"* she cried softly, as she fell into a chair on the upper deck of the yacht.

Jim had followed her outside and heard her words to Fred. He reached out his hand to introduce himself. "Well, brother, what do I have to do to get this girl to marry me? I am willing to do whatever it takes!" Jim declared.

Jim sat down beside Fred and they began to talk. Fred told him, "Susan doesn't want you to go through any hoops for her. She only wants to be certain you have a personal relationship with Jesus Christ like she does."

Jim immediately responded, "I could never have a relationship with God like Susan does. She is the purest, finest woman I have ever known in my life. I am just the opposite. I have lived a fast-paced lifestyle that is totally foreign to her way of thinking. But when I met her, I knew immediately I wanted to marry her. I was willing to change whatever I had to change to become her husband." Jim stopped and then added, "Why is this 'encounter' thing so important to her? Doesn't she know that all I want to do is to make her happy? I'll go to church with her. I'll see to it that the children go to Sunday School. What more do I need to do?"

Fred took a deep breath and breathed a prayer for wisdom. He suggested they move into the living room. When they were seated, he began to explain to Jim the meaning of salvation and the importance of being 'right with the Lord.' He deliberated about sin and forgiveness. As he talked, Jim looked down at his feet. The guilt of his sin began to weigh heavily upon his heart. He didn't understand all Fred was talking about; but he knew he had never confessed to Susan about his past. At that moment he realized he could not put that off any longer. Already, she had been blindsided by two of his friends. Violet had made him promise he would tell Susan everything so this would not happen again; but he had not kept that promise.

After a short time, he stopped Fred and told him he wanted Susan to be a part of this discussion. They called to her and she came down the steps. All three had somber countenances. Jim moved to the sofa and asked Susan to come and sit beside him. Then he engaged in what would be the most painful soliloquy of his life. He began to confess his sins to Fred and Susan. When Fred got up to leave, suggesting that they spend this time alone,

Jim protested. "No, Fred, I want you to be a witness to all I am saying. I need to tell you both and ask forgiveness. I see what I need to do, and I want to do it." Jim responded determinedly.

In the next few moments, reluctantly and very painfully, Jim opened up his heart, confessing his past sins — sometimes only in a whisper, at other times with tears and sobbing. One time he cried out, "Oh, God, why? Please forgive me!" The pictures that he painted were not pretty in any way. His confession revealed that he had thrown caution to the wind during his adult years. No drugs, but lots and lots of other things had filled his life. Susan was stunned and shocked!

In spite of all she was hearing from Jim's lips, however, Susan kept hearing his *heart* speak more loudly. She heard his regret, his shame, his remorse. She heard a man whose heart was broken because of his sin — a man who so deeply regretted he had made those choices and walked down those paths.

Finally, it seemed Jim's litany of sins had come to an end. There was silence except for intermittent sobs. Jim took Susan's hand and got down on his knees. "Oh, Susan, I don't expect you to marry me now. I should have told you all this sooner; but I knew I would probably lose you if I did. I could not fathom losing you. Now, the only thing that matters is for me to ask your forgiveness — forgive me for thinking a girl like you could ever want to marry a guy like me. Forgive me for not telling you these things sooner. Can you forgive me, Susan? I know you can't marry me now; but can you forgive me?" Jim was pleading with her now. His head fell on her knees.

Susan leaned over and took his head in her hands, kissing him on the ear. She cried and he cried. Then Jim lifted his head, got up and sat in a nearby chair. Immediately he bowed his head. Susan rose from her seat and walked over to the chair next to him. She sat down and took his hands in hers. She sat there in silence for a few moments. Then she spoke: "Look at me, Jim, please ... look at me. Yes, I am hurt and shocked and distressed about what you have told me. But I am so grateful to know a man like you who would confess his past and not try to fool the girl he wants to marry. Do you not know how much that means to me?" Susan tried to get him to look at her, but he was unable to look her in the eye. She continued anyway: "Jim, we are all sinners, in need of forgiveness for our own sins. That's why Jesus had to die on that cross."

Jim finally looked up at her with the saddest look she had ever seen. She wanted more than anything for him to hear what she was about to say. "Read my lips, Jim ... I . forgive . you!!"

"You didn't do all this to *me* — all sin is against God. The person you probably hurt the most after God is yourself. Perhaps forgiving yourself will be the hardest thing for you to do." He reached for her as they began to talk softly to each other.

After a time, Fred suggested they all get on their knees. He instructed Jim: "Now that you've asked our forgiveness, it's time to ask for God's forgiveness." He shared some thoughts about what Jim needed to do. Jim Hitchenson spent the next few moments praying and asking God to forgive him of his sins. He received Jesus Christ as his Savior and Lord.

He had *not* done this in order to get Susan to marry him, but to be able to live with himself. If Susan would still have him, that would be the most wonderful thing in the world. If she turned him down, he didn't know how he would make it without her; but he would know for certain he had done the right thing in asking Jesus to be his Savior and Lord. When the prayers were ended, Susan looked up at him and smiled. They helped each other up and stood facing each other. No words were necessary. Surely the Lord was in that place!

Susan threw her arms around him, kissing him gently. "I love you, Jim Hitchenson!" she declared, as Jim returned her embrace and kissed her once more.

After the kiss had ended, Jim stepped back a little, holding on to Susan's arms. He said, "I love you with all my heart and soul, Susan, but I have a special request. I don't want you to tell me whether you will still marry me until you've had some time to think, and I'm sure, pray about it. OK?"

Susan was taken aback at his words. She could not believe her ears. She stepped back and looked away for a moment. Tears filled her eyes. Turning back to him she sadly asked, "Is that really what you want, Jim?"

"Yes and no." Jim replied. "You know I can hardly stand the thought of being away from you again. But on the other hand, I don't want you to regret the decision you make about us. I've dumped a whole load on you today, baby. You need to be able to process it alone. I'm not going anywhere. I will be here, no matter how long it takes. I love you, Susan, and I always will."

Tears spilled down her face. She didn't want this separation, but she knew Jim was right. They did need time to think and pray. That is exactly what she would do. The two held each other for a long, long time — not wanting to ever let go. Jim kissed her fervently, then stepped back and said: "Go with her, Fred, and see that she gets home safely." Jim's lips formed a faint smile. "I entrust her to you and to God. I can assure you I'm going to do some praying myself."

Reluctantly, Susan allowed Fred to escort her from the boat. By the time they reached the end of the pier, she was sobbing. She felt as if her heart would break. Never had she felt so alone – so troubled – so fearful of leaving Jim. Was this the end? Was their relationship over? What was going to happen in the days ahead? "*Oh, God,*" she cried, as she got into Fred's car. "*You've got to help me or I won't make it. I want to do Your will, but this is so difficult. Have mercy on Jim and me, Oh, Lord. Pour out Your grace upon us both.*"

By this time, Fred was seated in the driver's seat. He backed out of the parking place and turned the car toward North Carolina. Susan would get her car later. She cried almost all the way to Morganton. It was a bittersweet day for her and Jim. Spiritually, he was no longer *lost*. He was a true believer in

Jesus Christ. But had she *lost* him as a fiancé this same day? She really wondered. The hurt in her heart seemed to extend from the top of her head to the bottom of her feet. Thoughts of regret were seizing her mind: *Oh, if only I had found out he wasn't a believer when we first met! I would have ended the relationship then. But I didn't, and here we are today! I know God was trying to speak to me through His Word that day I opened my Bible and saw the verse: "Unless the Lord builds the house, They labor in vain who build it." He was speaking to me, but I didn't listen. Look where it's gotten us both! Oh, God, please forgive me and help me."*

CHAPTER THIRTY
CHAPTER THIRTY

FOR the next month Susan wrestled with the biggest decision of her life – whether to marry Jim Hitchenson or not. The first two weeks were spent in Black Mountain at her parents' house. She sought counsel from her parents and Christian friends. She fasted and prayed. She studied God's Word and listened to sermons on her computer. She cried until she could cry no more. Her parents lovingly and compassionately listened to her and prayed with her every day. Her mother prayed constantly for Susan. She and Tom were deeply concerned about their precious daughter.

The hardest part for Susan was not being able to communicate with Jim. There were so many times she wanted to call and express her heart to him. She wanted desperately to know how Jim was doing. They had agreed not to talk during this month of separation; and she was going to abide by their agreement, as hard as it was.

At the beginning of the third week of separation, Susan traveled to her cousin's beach house in South Carolina. She quickly established a morning routine of praying, walking on the beach, and studying her Bible under her beach umbrella by the ocean. She loved studying God's Word as she watched the waves, one by one, come onto shore and flow back into the ocean. One could see the consistency of the waves as a representation of God's faithfulness. He was utterly trustworthy

— He had displayed His faithfulness to Susan all her life!

After lunch, she and Judy would pray, converse, and study the Bible some more. Susan's doubts began to diminish as the days went by. She loved Jim in spite of his past. After all, but for the grace of God, her life could have been more like his. She could not say, at this point, however, that marrying Jim was God's perfect will for her. She did not have God's peace! She could not go forward without it!

The last week her longing for Jim increased to the point she thought she could not stand being away from him any longer. She wondered what was happening in his life — what *he* was thinking at this point.

FOR Jim, dealing with his guilt was an ugly process. He knew God had forgiven him; but like Susan had thought, the hardest part *was* forgiving himself. How could he have lived like that for so long? He constantly battled his emotions and negative thinking. Often he found himself in the middle of the Circle of Regret! That first week he went back and forth between his parents' house and Violet and Dan's, seeking their wisdom and counsel. Violet and Dan were better able to understand his situation than his parents were. After all, they had been through a similar experience before they married.

With the first weekend approaching, Jim decided to sequester himself in his condo. He spent hours praying, studying the Bible and listening to recommended tapes. Violet called with a suggestion. She and Dan were good friends with a well-known Bible teacher in Atlanta. They had talked with him at length about Jim's situation. He volunteered to spend time with Jim if he would be agreeable to the idea. At Violet's urging, Jim agreed.

On Monday of the second week, this wonderful man of God began to spend several hours each week discipling and praying with Jim. As the days went by, Jim found himself emerging from the shell he had built around himself. He was gradually learning to accept the Lord's forgiveness and move forward. As a new Christian, he was taking 'baby steps;' but slowly he was beginning to understand the meaning and value of trusting and obeying the Lord! If only he knew what Susan would decide!

On Tuesday morning of the last week, he awoke with a heaviness he could not shake. In desperation, he dropped to the floor of his condominium, falling on his face before God. "Oh, God, help me. I don't think I can stand 'not knowing' any longer! I've got to know what Susan is thinking. I need to know her decision. If she isn't coming back to me, I want to know so that I can begin the awful process of getting over her. Oh, God, I love her so!"

Tears began to fall from Jim's eyes. He could not stop the flow. It was a time of release for him. He cried until the tears came no more — something he had never done before in his entire thirty years of life. Reaching up for a Kleenex on a table nearby, he wiped his eyes and blew his nose. He pulled himself up off the floor and fell into a nearby chair.

There was a lump beneath him; it was his Bible. He pulled his Bible out from under him. It fell out of his hand and dropped to the floor. Before he picked it up, something caught his attention. Some verses were underlined in red! He picked up his Bible. What he saw amazed him! Underlined in red were the verses Violet and Dan had urged him to memorize and practice: Proverbs 3: 5-6: "Trust in the Lord with all your heart, and lean not to your own understanding. In all your ways acknowledge Him, and He shall direct your paths." The commentary below read, "God will direct your paths, even when you don't understand what He is doing. Acknowledge Him in all your ways, and watch to see where He is leading you. His way is perfect." Jim was comforted by these words from God's Word.

THE month of separation was coming to an end. Susan still didn't have an answer. On the next to last day, she took a longer than usual walk on the beach. In her heart she knew she still wanted to marry Jim. She did not want to spend the rest of her life without him. But more than anything else, she wanted to do God's will. Her heart had been heavy during this month apart.

She went to her beach chair and sat down with a sigh. Bowing her head, she began to pray: *"Oh, Lord, if it is Your will for me to marry Jim, would You lift this burden and fill me with Your peace?! You know I want to marry him. Nevertheless, not my will but Thine be done."* It was a short prayer; but it was the only way she could pray at this moment.

She stared at the vast ocean and the distant horizon, marveling at how amazing it was that the Almighty God, who spoke the waters into existence, would hear the prayers of a little North Carolina girl sitting on an isolated beach! After a few minutes she got up and started strolling down the beach in the other direction. Unbelievably, all at once, the "peace that surpasses understanding"† began to flood into her soul. The heavy burden lifted. Her joy was returning! She was being *filled* with that peace she had prayed for!

God had heard and answered her prayer, and His answer was 'yes!' She fell to her knees and lifted her hands toward the heavens, crying out, *"Hallelujah! Thank you, O, Lord!"* She was free to marry Jim Hitchenson! God was the awesome God who would make their marriage a blessing in spite of the baggage from the past. He would be the builder of their home!

She got up and walked hurriedly toward her cousin's beach house. Another message of praise resounded over the waves: *"Praise God from Whom all blessings flow!"* She shouted through her tears of joy! Susan ran into her cousin's house almost yelling for her: "I've made my decision, Judy!" she called out. "I'm going to marry Jim!" Her cousin Judy quickly came from the bedroom and hugged Susan tightly. "I had an idea that would be your decision. I believe it's the right one for you!

Jim had come up with a plan for the end of the month. Susan had agreed. When her decision was made, Judy would call Jim. If the decision was a positive one, Jim would come to South Carolina as soon as possible. Immediately after hearing Susan's decision, her cousin began looking for Jim's number. When she found it, she picked up the phone and called him. He answered on the second ring. Susan could hear his response as he whooped and hollered and praised the Lord. She wanted to grab the phone and respond to him, but she couldn't break their agreement! She would have to wait. Their next conversation was to be face to face!

Susan walked down to the beach very early the next morning. She did not know the exact time Jim would arrive, but he would be there soon. She praised the Lord with every step she took. A few hours later as she was wading at the water's edge, she turned and glanced back at the road. Between the two houses was a vacant lot. She saw a man crossing the sand between the houses and coming her way. When she saw it was Jim, she immediately ran to greet him, calling out to him as she ran. He dropped his jacket in the sand and ran toward her. His arms closed around her. They stood silently embracing each other for several seconds. Then Susan stepped back, smiled her beautiful smile, and spoke the words Jim wanted to hear: "Oh, Jim. I told you a long time ago that now that I had found you, I wasn't about to let you go. Unless you've decided you want me to let you go, I intend to keep my word. I want to marry you, Jim Hitchenson!"

"Oh, Susan, oh, Susan, my beloved Susan," Jim replied, almost unable to contain his happiness. "You really are mine —

you really are mine!" He took her face in his hands and kissed her with all the passion of his soul. It was the beginning of a brand new chapter in their lives — a beautiful time for the two of them — a time of healing and hope. The Lord had answered their prayers. Praise His holy Name!

CHAPTER THIRTY-ONE
CHAPTER THIRTY-ONE

SUSAN spent the last day at her office thanking her employees and advising her replacement, John Travis. It was a happy-sad day for her — she loved her fellow workers. She loved her job at Hitchenson Enterprises. She loved Jim Hitchenson more. It was time to prepare for the upcoming wedding. Since Morganton was really 'home' for the Strasbourg's, the decision was made to have the wedding in their home church. It would not be a long trip for any of their close relatives. The friends and family from Atlanta would drive or fly.

Getting ready in a month was not going to be easy. Neither Susan nor Jim wanted to wait long to marry. Susan tried to keep it simple; but as so often happens, things seemed to mushroom. The guest list was completed. Friends were assembled to address the envelopes. The florist, photographer, and caterer were secured. Fred was, of course, to officiate at the wedding. Susan consulted with Jim about the wedding participants, the music and the ceremony. She wanted him to be pleased with everything that was planned.

After Jim and Susan had chosen the wedding attendants, Susan asked Violet to go shopping with her to find her wedding gown and bridesmaid dresses. Violet gave her whole-hearted approval to Susan's choice of gowns. She felt it was the "the perfect" wedding dress for Susan. She knew Jim would be "blown away" when he saw her in it. Susan loved it, too. She could hardly wait to wear it. Clover green was selected for the bridesmaid dresses. All three girls should look fantastic in that color.

Jim and Susan agreed to ask Susan's cousin Judy and Jim's cousin Al to be soloists at their wedding. Both had outstanding voices. The only thing left was an organist. The church had an organ, but had long since stopped using it. (Such were the customs of the 21st century.) To their surprise, the church had an organist among its members. She was delighted to be asked to play.

Two weeks before the wedding, Jim's parents were giving an elegant Announcement Party in Atlanta for family and friends. It would take Susan away from her wedding preparations; but it was a wonderful gift from Jim's parents. In looking forward to the event, Jim had an idea. He didn't know how Susan would feel about it. It seemed to be something he really wanted to do.

He called her late one night: "Sus, I hope you weren't asleep because I have something I want to discuss with you and get your opinion." He went on to say: "I've been thinking that I would like to have a pre-reception for our family and closest friends. I want so much to tell them what has happened in my life. They all know I've found the love of my life; I also want them to know that I've made my peace with God. What do you think?"

"Oh, Jim," Susan responded excitedly, "I think that is wonderful, wonderful! I love the idea that you would do that. It means more to me than you can imagine. What a great way to start the evening!"

"Okay, my love, then, it's settled. I'll start working on what I'm going to say. I'm sorry to wake you up. I promise I won't do that often," Jim concluded.

"You have my permission to awaken me anytime, Jim

Hitchenson. I belong to you and want to be available to you always." Susan responded.

"Good night, baby." Jim finished.

"Good night, my love." Susan answered as she hung up the phone. Then she thought to herself: I can't believe he is going to do that. How wonderful, wonderful, wonderful! I can hardly wait to see the looks on the faces of some of his old friends. They will be amazed! Then she prayed, "Oh, Lord, thank you, thank you for bringing Jim to this point and for bringing us together. What You have done for us separately and together is amazing!"

IT was the night of the Announcement Party. Jim had sent his plane to Morganton to bring Susan to Atlanta. She was waiting at Dan and Vi's for Jim's arrival. For this very special occasion she had purchased an elegant floor-length red organza gown. She hoped Jim would be pleased. When he arrived, he took one look at her and whistled. "Oh, Susan, you look fantastic!" He took her in his arms and kissed her.

You're the one, Jim. You know how I like you in a tux. Mr. Handsome himself. Oh, you look so good!" Susan exclaimed as she hugged him. Then she added, "You remember the first night we met when you came to my hotel room to pick me up for our Atlanta tour? When I opened the door and saw you with your shirt untucked and grinning from ear to ear, I fell so hard for you, I can't even express it. I thought I had never seen anyone so handsome and adorable in my whole life!"

Jim could not have been more thrilled with her words. "You didn't look too shabby yourself. But I must confess that I had already begun to fall for you before that. I think when you told me you liked me very much, I was smitten! I have loved you more every moment since then. I adore you, my Beautiful Prude!

If it were up to them, the two of them could have stayed right there and basked in the glory of their love. Knowing the parents and guests would not have understood, however, they postponed their private time until later. Violet and Dan were in the back of the house getting dressed, so Susan and Jim left without them. Once they were settled in Jim's Porsche, Jim started to get nervous about the coming event. Susan noticed his anxious demeanor.

"Are you alright?" Susan asked.

"Just a little nervous and uptight, I guess. I've never done anything like this before. It's hard to know how it's going to be received," Jim replied.

"Oh, I think it will be well received," Susan responded. "I know you will handle it just perfectly. You always do. That's one of the things I love about you. You seem to always know the right thing to say." He thanked her, and she tried to get his mind on other things as they rode to the engagement party.

They soon arrived and went straight to the pre-reception room. The microphone and speaker's stand were set up for them. When the guests began to arrive, Jim and Susan greeted them warmly. Since there were no refreshments offered, everyone simply gathered in small groups. Some of them were whispering to each other, speculating on what this special pre-reception was about. Most of them could not possibly have guessed what was about to transpire.

Soon it was time to begin. Susan and Jim walked to the podium. Jim looked handsome in his tuxedo. Susan looked gorgeous in her lovely red gown enhanced by the beautiful diamond jewelry Jim had given her as an engagement present. Jim's voice over the mike got the attention of nearly everyone. "Hello, friends and family. Susan and I would like to thank you for coming early tonight. We chose you to attend this small gathering because you are all so special to us. Everyone here is either related to us or is a very close friend. You mean more to us than you will ever know."

"First of all, you know that this is one of the most exciting and wonderful nights of our lives," Jim continued as he reached out and pulled Susan closer to him. "There is not a happier man alive tonight than I am. For Susan to have agreed to marry me is nothing short of a miracle. You all know by now that she is beautiful inside and out — and she is the most wonderful thing that has ever happened to me. I have to pinch myself some times to believe she is really going to be my wife."

Susan moved in front of Jim and lifted her head so she could speak through the microphone: "But I am and I can hardly wait!" Everyone laughed and clapped at the same time. Jim grinned and kissed her on the cheek as he pulled her closer to him. Then Jim moved over a little and stood erect.

He continued: "I've asked you to come tonight because, not only have I found the love of my life — the one I want to spend the rest of my life with — I have also found something else. And I wanted to tell you this in person." Jim paused a minute and added, "That something else is peace with God." He saw and heard a shuffling in the crowd.

Susan moved over so he could have the entire podium. "A few weeks ago, Susan told me of her concern about our differing lifestyles. She was afraid that might mean our beliefs and values were not the same. She told me she did not want to lock me into a relationship which I would later regret. At first, I really couldn't understand what she was trying to say. But Susan reminded me of Violet's and Dan's experience. I began to reflect on those differences they had to face. As I did, I saw clearly the things I needed to deal with. The weight of the baggage I was carrying around from the past became a heavy burden I could not shake. Violet had wisely told me that I should be truthful with Susan about my days of 'rather wild living,' I guess you could call it." Everyone laughed when he said that. Jim looked at

Susan and she nodded in agreement with a smile on her face.

"Two weeks ago, on a morning I shall never forget, I came to the realization that I had some things I needed to share before I could ever expect Susan to marry me. And I knew that if I were truthful with her, she might not want to marry me. Whether she still wanted to marry me was not the issue any more. The issue was whether I could live with myself if I didn't make things right with her and with God. I came to the conclusion that I could not.

"In front of Susan and the minister who is going to marry us, I owned up to the things I felt I must share from my past. Many tears were shed. When I finished my confessional, I begged Susan's forgiveness. Then the minister, Susan and I all knelt there on my boat. He led me in a prayer. I asked God's forgiveness for turning my back on Him. In that time on my knees, I received God's forgiveness and cleansing, and Jesus Christ became my Savior and Lord.

"You may think I went through this process just to get Susan to marry me. But that would not be the truth. By the time I finished confessing, I didn't think she *would* marry me. I went through this process because I could no longer live the way I was living. That lifestyle was never what I wanted — I just thought I did. What I really always wanted — and you can ask mom and Vi — was to find the love of my life, marry her and have lots of children. When I couldn't seem to find the woman I wanted to marry, I turned aside and made some really bad choices.

"Since my lovely fiancée is standing here by my side, you already know that she forgave me that morning. I told her that I understood that didn't mean she would still marry me; and I have to admit I was not at all sure she would. But in the end, she told me that when she found me, she never intended to let me go. If it was okay with me, she was going to hold on to me forever. That was absolutely incredible news to me!" Everyone clapped as he reached over and kissed her again.

"Tonight I want to go one step further in this journey I'm now on. I would like to ask forgiveness from each of you. I am sorry that it has taken me so long to realize what a futile existence I was living. I am sorry for any way in which I have impacted your life negatively. I have come to realize in these past weeks that nothing is more important than making our peace with God — nothing is more important than a right relationship with Him.

"So tonight, I wanted you to know what has happened in my life. No longer do I want to do things *my* way; I want to do them *God's* way!" He smiled at Susan and reached over to take her hand. Then he continued. "If you are a praying person, please pray for Susan and me as we go forward from this day. We do so with God's help. If you want to talk with either or both of us after the honeymoon, please do. We always want to be available to our friends and family." He paused a moment, looked around at his audience and smiled. "That's all I wanted to say, tonight, folks. Thank you so much for giving me this opportunity to share with you. Now, let's all go into the reception and have a wonderful time. We'll see you in the ballroom." Jim turned to Susan and hugged her tightly.

"You were absolutely awesome!" Susan told him when he released her. "Did you see their faces? They were awestruck and spellbound. You were wonderful. I'm so glad you decided to do this." By this time Violet and Dan were on the platform hugging both of them. Others began to come forward. Some didn't know what to say, but they tried. Each seemed to admire Jim for having the courage to do what he had just done. No one seemed turned off by his words. Jim was relieved. He had obeyed God; and now He must leave things in God's hands.

As they came down from the platform with Dan and Violet, an old friend of Jim's who had been invited at the last minute stopped them all. "What you just did, Jim, was one of the most amazing things I've ever seen. You will never know the impact it's going to have on the city of Atlanta!" Jim was stunned, but thanked him profusely. Then the guy continued. "You probably don't know it, Jim, but I am an alcoholic — a sober for six years alcoholic — but still that's what I will always be. At a retreat for alcoholics, I received Jesus Christ into my life, and things have never been the same. I learned then that if a transformation happens in our lives and we don't share it, people will always wonder about us. If we share it, we take the risk we may back slide; but the risk is worth it. You never know who's on the brink of disaster when you share how God can change a life. Thanks, Jim."

"Oh, thank you, Tom. That is very encouraging." Jim eagerly responded as he and Susan walked into the ballroom.

CHAPTER THIRTY-TWO
CHAPTER THIRTY-TWO

IMMEDIATELY they were bombarded by the many guests at the party. Susan was enthralled with all the gorgeous flowers and lighted trees. It looked like a beautiful garden. Ice sculptures in many shapes and sizes were filled with lavish bouquets of elegant blooms. The food was displayed delectably. The female guests were outfitted in the latest fashions. She had never seen anything like this in Morganton! The night was going to be more than she could ever have hoped for! Jim had already made it unbelievably wonderful!

Since Jim did not want liquor at this party, sparkling grape juice and ginger ale could be found in the flowing fountains set in each corner of the banquet hall. Chocolate strawberries, miniature pecan pies, and tiny crème Brule's were in abundance, too. All were favorites of Susan and Jim's. There was a roast beef station as well as another with varied types of meats including ribs and pork tenderloin. A station with delicious dips was always busy. The boiled shrimp station was obviously very popular. A delightfully displayed assortment of fruits and cheeses rounded out the full menu. No one would go away hungry, for sure.

About an hour into the event, Jim's dad went to the microphone and proposed a toast to the happy couple. He then asked to say a few words. He called his wife up to his side, and then asked Susan and Jim, Dan and Violet to stand on the other side.

"Tonight is a wonderful night for us all. Ruth and I are about to pop our buttons. Our daughter has just married a fantastic guy, and our son is about to marry a fantastic girl. And look at these two couples. If Ruth and I aren't going to have beautiful grandchildren, my name isn't James Hitchenson!" Everyone laughed as they clapped in agreement.

He continued. "This is Jim and Susan's big night!" Violet and Dan respectfully went back to their seats. Mr. Hitchenson turned to Jim and Susan. "Jim, we want you to know that we could not be more thrilled that you have chosen Susan. We loved her from the first minute we met her — and we understand you did, too." Jim shook his head affirmatively, and pulled Susan toward him as the audience laughed. "Ruth decided that first night, that if Jim didn't ask her to marry him, she was going to hog-tie him till he did!" A roar went up from the crowd. Jim and Susan just smiled. "Susan, we want to thank you for agreeing to marry our son. He is one fine son; we are so proud of him. We know you are going to be a wonderfully happy couple with a lasting marriage.

Now, if you will please come over here a moment, we have a little something for you." Immediately, someone brought up an easel covered in a burgundy cloth. Jim slowly pulled the cloth away revealing a fabulous lake lot on Lake Lanier. It was filled with mature trees. Susan and Jim both gasped.

"Oh, my, dad. I can't believe you did this!" Jim exclaimed as he looked at the picture of the lot on Lake Lanier he had always wanted to own. For years he had dreamed of buying it and building a beautiful home there, but the owner wouldn't sell it.

"How did you get them to sell it to you, Dad," Jim blurted out. "I wasn't sure they would ever let it go."

Jim's Dad grinned. "Well, they sold it to me when I told them it was for you and Susan! Mom and I want you to have it.

Here is the deed for the lot. Now go build the home of your dreams and give us lots of grandchildren!" He laughed as he gave Jim an envelope.

Susan and Jim hugged Jim's parents as the crowd started clapping loudly. After exchanging their love and appreciation, Jim went to the mike. "Folks, I don't have words for this. For dad and mom to give us this premier lot on Lake Lanier is unbelievable." He turned to his parents again and said, "Please know that we are both overwhelmed and thrilled with this gracious gift. And know that there are no two people who would rather live on this lake than Susan and me. We are Lake People — boat people — water birds, if you will. We are going to love it. Thank you, thank you, thank you." Susan echoed his words and they hugged his parents again.

Jim then spoke to the crowd, inviting them all to the wedding. "If you can't come to North Carolina for the wedding, please come see us after our honeymoon. We'll be in my condo during the building process." He smiled and pulled Susan closer. "Thank you for sharing this wonderful time of our lives with us. God bless you all."

The evening had turned out better than Jim and Susan could have imagined. God was so good! The most wonderful thing was the peace they were both experiencing these days — the "peace that surpasses all understanding" – God's perfect peace through His Son Jesus Christ.

CHAPTER THIRTY-THREE

CHAPTER THIRTY-THREE

AT last it was their wedding day! The sun was shining brightly. If the day had been cloudy, Susan and Jim would not have noticed. Love reigned supreme in their hearts this day.

The church was packed. Many from Atlanta had made the trip. The North Carolina folks were there in great numbers. The sanctuary had never looked prettier! Lovely bouquets of flowers were framed by glowing s-shaped candelabra. Adorning the unique candelabra, were white roses, calla lilies, Casablanca lilies and baby's breath intermingled with greenery and taffeta ribbon. Attached to every third pew was a small bouquet of white miniature calla lilies, roses and greenery. Clover-green taffeta ribbon tied the bouquets to the pew clips. The taffeta streamers fell from each bouquet.

On the platform in front of a massive bouquet of white flowers was the antique kneeling bench that belonged to Susan's Grammy Jane. Lovely white pillows were attached for kneeling. Susan and Jim would be kneeling there at the end of the service.

Melodious music resounded throughout the sanctuary. Playing the prelude and wedding music were an organist, two violinists and a cellist.

Susan's cousin Judy sang *In Christ Alone* by the Getty's. Jim's cousin Al sang Stephen Curtis Chapman's, *I Will Be Here.* The two soloists joined in a duet to sing the wedding song Steve

Green made famous, *Household of Faith*. What a delightful musical concert it was!

It was time for the processional. The organist began to play. From the right side of the altar came the minister, groom and groomsmen. Jim's dad was his best man. Bill Sullivan and Hal Kearney were the groomsmen. They all took their places in front of the platform.

Tom Strasbourg and Susan were standing just outside the back door of the sanctuary, waiting their turn to walk down the aisle. Susan turned to her dad and said softly: "Dad, you are the very best dad in the world! I want to thank you for all you've done for me. So much of what I am today I credit to your teaching and example. I love you, Dad. Don't ever forget that!"

With tears in his eyes, Susan's dad could hardly speak. "You are the very best *daughter* in the world, Susie. You are a beautiful reflection of God's glory! It is my prayer that you will have as wonderful a marriage as your mother and I have had. Jim loves you, sweet girl, and I know he'll take good care of you. Just don't ever forget your ole mom and dad. We'll always be here for you."

The first bridesmaid was almost to the altar. Her long clover-green satin A-line gown had a beaded neckline and spaghetti straps. Each bridesmaid carried a bouquet of white roses, calla lilies and dahlias tied with taffeta ribbon which matched their dresses. Violet was the second bridesmaid. The green dress was the color of her eyes. She looked lovely in her bridesmaid's dress. The third attendant was Betsy Markham Wheeler, Susan's matron of honor. She had been a dear friend of Susan's from childhood.

When Betsy had taken her place at the altar, a trumpet sounded from the balcony. It was the signal for Susan to enter the sanctuary. What a gorgeous bride she was! At the edge of each shoulder were lace cap sleeves lined with white satin ribbon. The same pattern was picked up in her veil atop her fashionable swept up hairdo, and in her long flowing train. The diamond earrings and necklace Jim had given her were a perfect complement to her exquisite Alencon lace gown. She carried a bouquet of roses, calla lilies and lilies of the valley. Green taffeta ribbon was interspersed throughout her bouquet, with streamers floating below. She could have been on the cover of any bridal magazine. There was no way to describe how elegant she looked.

It would not be the dress, however, that her wedding guests would notice most. As the guests stood in her honor, what they saw was a radiantly beautiful brunette who was very much in love both with the man waiting at the end of the aisle and with Jesus Christ, her Lord. As she and her dad approached the altar and came into Jim's full view, he could hardly stand in one spot. His wide grin could not have conveyed the absolute joy he felt as at last, he saw his bride. Susan Strasbourg was really 'his;' and at that moment, he wanted to dance and sing, and shout 'Hallelujah!' Instead, he whispered, "I love you," as she and her dad stepped into place beside him. She leaned forward and mouthed the words back to him.

It seemed like eons before her daddy gave her away and she placed her arm in Jim's. As she did, Jim looked down at her and said, "You look gorgeous, Beautiful Prude!"

She grinned and said, "So do you!" They were brought back to attention by the minister's words. They followed him up on the platform where the remainder of the ceremony was to take place. They would always remember some of the words Fred shared during the ceremony: "Woman was not taken from man's head to rule over him, or from his feet to be trampled on by him. Rather, she was taken from his side, from under his arm, to be a lover and companion all his days." Later they would agree that was just the way they wanted their relationship to be.

As they knelt on the kneeling bench to pray, Jim's big hands tightly grasped Susan's smaller ones. They had asked Dan to pray for them; he prayed a beautiful prayer and Susan cried.

These were tears of joy and thankfulness for all God had done in their lives in such a short time.

It was finally time for the minister to pronounce them man and wife. Jim couldn't wait to kiss Susan. He found her lips as Fred was speaking. Everyone clapped. As the clapping subsided, the minister did get to say one thing the audience heard: "I now present to you Mr. and Mrs. James Martin Hitchenson, Jr." What beautiful words to Jim and Susan's ears!

At the bottom of the steps the happy couple moved first to the right of the podium. They reached out to Susan's mother first. Susan kissed her mother on the cheek, hugged her dad, and Jim did the same. Then they moved to the left and followed suit with Jim's parents. It was a very special time for both families.

When the glowing couple had exited the sanctuary, Jim took Susan in his arms and kissed her over and over. He kept whispering, "You are mine, Beepie, you are mine. You are really mine." Between kisses, Susan tried to say, "Yes, I am." But it didn't matter if she couldn't get a word in; the truth was, she *was* his now — now and forever. She was Susan Hitchenson; and that fact was one she would always love to acknowledge. They were not 'unequally yoked.' She had wanted God to build their house, and He had begun to do so this very day. Yes, "the Lord would build their house; their labors would not be in vain."†

There was no way Jim Hitchenson could have explained his feelings that day to an onlooker. The joy he felt was boundless; he thought he was going to explode with happiness. He had married the girl of his dreams — the love of his life — and he could hardly believe it! All he wanted to do for the rest of his life was to show her just how much he loved her. She was and always would be his 'better half.' He intended to treat her like that forever. He knew he didn't deserve her, but she loved him unconditionally. *Wasn't that what God did for us?* Jim thought to himself. At that moment he couldn't have imagined that their message to the world would be summed up by John 3:16 † —

the greatest story of unconditional love ever told!

Jim and Susan left the reception in a white limousine. The first stop was Susan's aunt's house. Their plan was to change clothes and depart for Lake Lure. Jim was in a bedroom across the hall from Susan. As he was tucking in his casual shirt, he suddenly made a decision: "I *want to see my bride!*"

Moving quickly across the hall, he knocked on the door and called out, "Mrs. Hitchenson?" Susan was surprised that he had come so soon. But, joyfully realizing it was her *husband* knocking at her door, Susan's response was exactly what he wanted to hear. "Come in, Mr. Hitchenson," she called out to him. He slowly opened the door. A new day had dawned in their lives. The Lord had started building their house! It would be an example of God's amazing grace!

THE END

PERSONAL NOTE

PERSONAL NOTE

I began writing this novella several years ago and have revised it many times. In the past, the bulk of my writing has been non-fiction. After praying for months about publishing the novella, in January of 2014, I specifically asked for the Lord's guidance about going forward. The answer unexpectedly and miraculously came from the Olivia Kimbrell Press™ the very next day, in response to an inquiry about the company. So, with much excitement, I am presenting for your reading pleasure my first Christian novella, *A Beautiful Reflection.*

It is my desire to show that living in this modern age of "anything goes," does not mean that a woman with deep Spiritual convictions cannot survive and even thrive! I hope to see women challenge today's worldly lifestyles by living life from a Biblical worldview — refusing to compromise their convictions no matter how tempting it may be. I also pray that readers will more fully understand the problems in being "unequally yoked."

My prayer is that God will use this book for His glory in your life!

In Christ,

Sarah O. Maddox

Reader's Guide

Reader's Guide

SUGGESTED luncheon discussion group questions for *A Beautiful Reflection.*

In bringing those He ministered to into an understanding of the truth, our Lord used fiction in the form of parables to illustrate very real truths. In the same way, we can minister to one another by the use of fictional characters and situations to help us to reach logical, valid, cogent, and very sound conclusions about our real lives here on this earth.

While the characters and situations in this story are fictional, I pray that these extended parables can help readers come to a better understanding of truth as Christ proclaimed it. Please prayerfully consider the questions that follow, consult scripture, and pray upon your conclusions.

Susan Strasbourg felt apprehensive about attending her company's national convention.

1. Have you ever attended an event where your convictions were tested?

2. When Jim Hitchenson paid attention to Susan that first night, what challenges did that present to her?

3. How well do you think Susan handled Jim's obvious interest in her?

4. How do you feel about "love at first sight"?

Read Psalm 51:6 and take a time of prayer; then answer these questions.

5. In the story, what were some warning signs Susan should have heeded on this "journey with Jim?"

6. Why is it important to spend time getting to know a prospective mate and fully understanding his spiritual beliefs before making a lifetime commitment?

In the story, Jim and Susan witness events that take place in the lives of Dan and Violet.

7. Why do you think Jim and Susan did not apply what happened to Dan and Violet to their own situation, until it was nearly too late?

Read the verses in *II Corinthians 6:14* and *Psalms 127:1* and take a time of prayer. In the story, the Holy Spirit stopped Susan from moving forward with her relationship with Jim until she determined whether Jim truly was a genuine believer in Christ.

8. Has the Holy Spirit ever stopped you from moving in a direction that was wrong for you?

Read Jeremiah 29: 11-14 and take a time of prayer. In the story, Susan earnestly sought God's will throughout the month of separation from Jim.

9. How do you go about finding God's will for your life?

Most of us know at least one person who is married to a non-believer.

10. What are some of the justifications Christian women often state for marrying a non-Christian?

11. What are some reasons "unequally yoked" couples often have marital problems?

In the story, Jim courageously shares his salvation experience with his friends and family before the Announcement Party.

12. Why is it often harder to witness to family and friends than acquaintances or strangers?

Read I Corinthians 6: 18-20 then take a time of prayer. Consider how few modern women, even professing Christian young women, share Susan's convictions about premarital sex.

13. What can you do to encourage purity in your daughters and/or granddaughters?

ABOUT THE AUTHOR
ABOUT THE AUTHOR

SARAH O. MADDOX was born in Kentucky and reared in Mississippi as the daughter of a Southern Baptist pastor. She has lived most of her life in Tennessee as helpmate to Roland, mother to their two children, grandmother, Bible teacher, writer, and author. She has been actively involved in local and national ministries all through the years.

Her first book published in 1999 and co-authored with Patti Webb, *A Mother's Garden of Prayer* was written as a guide for mothers and grandmothers in praying for their children and grandchildren in accordance with God's Word. *A Mother's Garden of Prayer Journal* soon followed in 2000. Her second book, *A Woman's Garden of Prayer*, also co-authored with Mrs. Webb, was released in 2002. This gift book was written to encourage women to cultivate intimacy with God through prayer. *A Woman's Garden of Prayer Journal* accompanies this book. In October of 2004, Sarah's first independently authored title, *Five Things I Did Right and Five Things I Did Wrong in Raising Our Children* was published.

It has been Sarah's desire to inspire and motivate young women to be faithful to their Lord, their husbands, their children, and their churches. For many years her main emphasis was teaching and encouraging women to pray for their children.

Underlying all of her messages has been her fervent belief that we should never give up on our children – never give up on God!

Sarah resides in Tennessee with her husband. near her daughter's family. Her life verse is Jeremiah 32:17: "Ah, Lord God! Behold, You have made the heavens and the earth by Your great power and outstretched arm. There is nothing too hard for You." (NJKV)

You can contact Sarah at sarah.maddox@somrm.com or find her on Facebook.

ACKNOWLEDGEMENTS
ACKNOWLEDGEMENTS

I want to thank my wonderful husband, Roland Maddox, for allowing me to spend so much time on the computer writing my books. I especially appreciate his critique of *A Beautiful Reflection.*

One of the inspirations for this book was my husband's involvement in *True Love Waits*, in its very inception at LifeWay Christian Resources in Nashville, TN. The two young men at LifeWay who conceived and developed *True Love Waits*, had not been able to find the funding to produce this program. They came to my husband, an executive at LifeWay with their dilemma. Roland was able to secure the initial funding to begin this outstanding program. What a blessing it has been to see how this God-inspired program has impacted so many lives!

God has been so good to allow me to work with Gregg and Hallee Bridgeman. I especially want to thank Gregg for his expertise, his graciousness and patience, and for the time and effort he gave to my first novel. I have truly been blessed!

BIBLIOGRAPHY
BIBLIOGRAPHY

Following are references to scrpture used in this book in the order they appeared. All verses of scripture are transcribed from the New King James Version (NKJV) translation of the Holy Bible :

Matthew 12:34b

How can you, being evil, speak good things? For out of the abundance of the heart the mouth speaks.

2 Timothy 1:7

For God has not given us a spirit of fear, but of power and of love and of a sound mind.

Psalm 127:1 (used multiple times)

Laboring and Prospering with the Lord

A Song of Ascents. Of Solomon.

Unless the Lord builds the house,

They labor in vain who build it;

Unless the Lord guards the city,

The watchman stays awake in vain.

2 Corinthians 6:14

Do not be unequally yoked together with unbelievers. For what fellowship has righteousness with lawlessness? And what communion has light with darkness?

I John 4:4

You are of God, little children, and have overcome them, because He who is in you is greater than he who is in the world.

Philippians 4:13

I can do all things through Christ * who strengthens me.

* Many texts also read *Him* who.

Philippians 4:7

and the peace of God, which surpasses all understanding, will guard your hearts and minds through Christ Jesus.

John 3:16

For God so loved the world that He gave His only begotten Son, that whoever believes in Him should not perish but have everlasting life.